AMISH MYSTERY: PLAIN SECRETS

ETTIE SMITH AMISH MYSTERIES BOOK 17

SAMANTHA PRICE

Print ISBN 978-1-925689-62-4

CHAPTER 1

SEETHING WITH RAGE, Selena drove up to the caretaker's house hoping he'd be home. Now she regretted not contacting him sooner, but the past years had been nothing short of hectic.

She parked her car close to the small house at the address she'd programmed into the vehicle's GPS, jumped out and looked at the place. The house was nicely kept, white, with red roof and red window frames. The red was a little bold for an Amish person's house, Selena considered. A wide porch wrapped around two sides of the house and two large white wooden chairs sat neatly between two windows, turned slightly toward one another. A small round table stood between them. It was the kind of cottage that would feature in a magazine as a perfect weekend-getaway spot. If only her grandfather's house looked as nice, but thanks to this care-taker, it didn't.

With her hands curled into fists, she summoned her courage and marched over and knocked on the door. A minute later, a tall Amish man opened it, and she stepped back in fright at his looming presence. A split second was all

1

it took for him to look her up and down, and then a smile swept across his angular facial features. Before she could utter a disapproving word in regard to his care-taking failures, he stepped outside without a word and strode past her. Selena watched in amazement while he turned his face up to the sky.

"*Denke, Gott.* I didn't expect you to answer me so soon." He turned his head and locked eyes with her. "I was praying for the right woman and here you are. You're perfect." When she stepped to the edge of the porch, confused, his gaze dropped to her clothes. "Although, you're not Amish, which might pose a problem if you're not willing to join my community."

She stared at him. Her mother had told her Amish people were barking mad, and Selena had figured it was an exaggeration, but now she had the evidence before her. Although, when she'd met her grandfather back when she was eight, he hadn't seemed crazy. "I've got no idea what you're talking about. I'm Selena Lehman. Abner Troyer was my grandfather."

"That's excellent! You don't look like him at all." Using hand gestures, he said, "He had brown eyes and white hair, and you have the most amazing green eyes." He stepped closer placing his hand down by his side. "They're quite remarkable. They go so well with your light brown hair. It's not golden brown, it's more of a ... I don't know what it's similar to. I like it." He smiled at her revealing his straight white teeth.

This was a perfect looking man to go with his perfect looking house, but what about her place? Where was that in his list of priorities? "Are you John Yoder?" She was taken aback by the man's behavior; now she hoped this man *wasn't* the caretaker of the house she was soon to take possession of.

"There are four John Yoders in the community. Are you

looking for the John Yoder who's looking after your grandfather's house?"

"Yes." She heaved a sigh of relief. "Where can I find him?"

"That's me." He pointed to himself. "Officially I'm John Yoder, but to save the John Yoder confusion in the community, I go by my middle name, Gabriel. You can call me Gabriel, or even Gabe if you'd like."

"I'll stick with Gabriel. Like the angel." She hoped he'd be offended, but he appeared not to notice.

"Good. I thought you'd come eventually. I haven't minded looking after the place."

"Looking after?" The anger within her cranked up a notch. "I just drove there and saw people living in it." She stared at him knowing he'd offer some lame excuse. Was he pocketing the rent money—keeping it for himself?

"I figure you can ..."

"You don't even know me, so you can stop figuring anything. Besides, to set you straight, I'm not your 'right woman' either. I came here because you're supposed to be caretaker of Abner's house. I went there just now to find a houseful of screaming children."

"Ah. You've met the King family." His silly grin was back.

Selena sighed. "Whoever they are, they shouldn't be in my house."

"Why?"

Wasn't he listening? "It's *my* house."

He raised a finger in the air. "Ah, that's not quite correct. I'm left as caretaker until it's transferred to you, and I do believe your *onkel*—"

"Grandfather."

"Yes, your grandfather left it to you but you can't have it until your thirtieth birthday. I'm led to believe that's not for quite some years. Until then, I have the entire sayso over the place." His gaze traveled up and down her, having another good look. "You don't look anywhere near thirty and I'm a good judge of age. Also, I have the documents relating to the house to tell me what age you are." He gave a small chuckle at his own words. "You're not married yet, are you?"

She crossed her arms at her waist, not liking the weird stranger at all. He was tall, and technically he was handsome with his sun-kissed skin and beautiful teeth, but he was acting goofy and his mannerisms matched her assumption of him.

It was tiresome after her long drive to have to explain herself to a stranger, but if she didn't she'd have no chance of getting those people out of her house. "I know what the will said. I'm getting married soon—that's why I'm here to see my house."

The smile left his lips. "You're getting married?"

She nodded.

He looked up to the sky. "Why? Why test me like this?"

Selena cringed. "Look. I just want the people out of my house. I'm here to see if I'll sell it after I marry, or lease it."

"Wait a minute. I have to get used to the idea we're not getting married." He hung his head.

Selena froze, not knowing what to do. Were all the Amish as odd as her mother had said? She dared not speak again until he did.

He placed his thumb and forefinger on the bridge of his nose and she saw his lips moving as though he were whispering to God. Then he placed his hand by his side and raised his head. "Okay. Now, you said you're getting married to … someone?"

After a frustrated huff, Selena tried to speak, but couldn't. This man was nothing like the Amish people she'd pictured in her mind's eye. She never expected there to be anyone with his looks in the community. She wondered what he'd be like if he hadn't been raised Amish. She cleared her throat and reminded herself why she was there. "That's not the point. I'm devastated about there being people in the house adding wear and tear when you're supposed to be the caretaker. Are you responsible for allowing them there?"

He nodded for a moment and then said, "Yes, I am, but you have to understand there are taxes and repairs that need to be met and paid for. Sometimes, it's not good for a house to be empty for years. A house needs to be lived in or it will fall into ruin. A house needs to be loved, just like a man."

She ignored that last remark. He didn't look like a man who'd be short of female attention. "Oh, didn't my grandfather provide money for the upkeep?"

He stared at her for a moment. "No." He took a step closer. "Are you really getting married?"

She looked up at him towering over her and wanted to back away; instead, she stood her ground. "Yes."

"I can show you through the house. The Kings won't mind. Did you tell them who you were?"

"No. I was too shocked. I didn't go inside. I mean, I didn't even knock on the door. I saw people running around and kids hanging out the windows and all kinds of carrying on. I looked up your address and came here."

"Yes, good." He stood staring at her, his dark eyes crinkling at the corners.

"When could you show me through?"

"Now, if you'd like. I'll just hitch the buggy. It won't take long."

"We can go now?" she asked.

"That's right."

She wasn't going to argue. "Good. We can go in my car." She knew from what her mother told her the Amish could ride in cars, they just couldn't own them or drive them.

He looked over at her car and then brushed his hand over

5

his head, sweeping his almost-shoulder-length dark hair over to one side. "I'm not going in *that.*"

Her mouth fell open. It was one of her fiancé's new cars, a Mercedes—sleek and black and new. Most people gave her compliments whenever she drove up in it. No one had ever acted like him toward it, as though it was detestable. "Why not?"

He held his chiseled chin high. "You can come with me."

"In a buggy?"

"That's right. It'll take me two minutes." Without waiting for an answer, he strode off toward the barn.

Anger had given her courage, but now the adrenaline let-down made her legs feel like jelly and she sat down on the stone steps of the porch. From there, she heard him calling out to what she thought must be a horse, and then she heard some noises. Two minutes—plus thirteen—later, he drove a horse and buggy around from behind the barn.

"Let's go," he called out. By the time she reached the buggy, he'd put on a hat. "Wait." He jumped out of the buggy and hurried to her side and took hold of her hand. "I'll help you."

She tugged her hand away annoyed at being touched by the stranger. "I'm quite capable of getting into a buggy."

His smile didn't falter at her angry words and he watched her until she was seated. Then he walked back around and climbed into the driver's seat.

If Selena could get past the strange man sitting beside her, she didn't mind having a ride in a buggy while she was in Amish country. This is how her mother had traveled until she left the Amish at eighteen. "And are these people on a lease?"

"No, they just pay when they can."

"Pay when they can?" Selena screeched clutching at her throat. This was getting worse by the minute.

"They pay, they do pay. You see, Molly's been sick and often Matt has to miss work to look after her. It all works out in the end." He glanced over at her. "If they weren't in it, there wouldn't be anybody and there'd be no money for the upkeep."

Simmering with anger, she sat still. She'd assess the situation when she got there. It sounded more and more like it would be easier to sell, but what state would the place be in? She had to keep all this from Eugene. He was under enough stress with his job already.

"You seem upset."

"I am. I'm worried about what my fiancé will think."

He pushed his hat back on his head. "It'll be okay. You'll see."

She gave him a sideways glance wondering why her grandfather had chosen him to look after his house until she met the terms of the will. "You knew my grandfather well?"

"Yes, very much so. He and I got along nicely. I was always over there listening to all his stories. It was sad he died in jail like he did."

"What?" Had she heard right? "Wait a minute. Did you say he died in …? in … jail?" She stared at him, carefully watching his lips, so she wouldn't mistake his answer.

He frowned at her. "You didn't know?"

"Jail?"

Gabriel nodded. "Yes, he was in jail."

"What for?"

"Nothing much." He shook his head.

"What?" she repeated, now losing what little she had left of her patience.

"He admitted to killing someone, but we all know he didn't do it. It could've even been an accident, but—"

She immediately was sick to the stomach. "Stop the buggy."

7

He didn't waste time pulling the buggy off to one side of the country road. She jumped out and started walking through the grass at the roadside with her hand over her stomach. What would Eugene say when he found out her grandfather was a criminal? Being a lawyer with high hopes of becoming a judge, he'd been pleased she'd had no criminals in her family history. They'd had a conversation about it. He'd ended his last relationship when he found out the girl's father had spent some months in jail for a white-collar crime. That was just fraud, nothing like a murder. If he found out about Abner he'd surely dump her and marry someone more suited.

"Are you alright, Selena?"

She heard Gabriel's voice from behind her. "Yes." She snapped at him and then was immediately sorry. He'd done nothing wrong and was trying to be helpful. She swung around. "I'm sorry. I'm just tired and angry, and now I hear about a murder. It's too much."

"He didn't do it." The stupid grin was back plastered all over his face.

"You said he admitted it."

"That's right."

She fought back tears. Her life as she knew it, was over. "He must've done it."

He looked thoughtful. "I know that's how it sounds."

She shook her head. "Just give me a moment." She turned around and walked some more, wondering what to do. Until she found out more she'd have to keep it secret from Eugene or their perfect life would unravel faster than she'd driven his new Mercedes on the open road. She inhaled deeply. *Keep it together.* When she swung around, she saw Gabriel sitting patiently in the buggy. She'd really have to try to be nicer to him. He was patient even when she was rude to him and that made her feel awful.

"You okay?" he called out again as she walked back to him.

"Yes." Once she climbed back beside him, she said, "Could you please tell me all you know about this crime?"

He took off his hat, licked his lips and then ran a hand through his hair. "Someone was run down in the street."

"Like a hit-and-run?"

"Yes. And, many years later, Abner admitted to it."

"How many years are we talking?"

He shook his head. "So long ago. Twenty or thirty years, or something."

"He can't have been in jail that long. I visited him when I was about eight in the house I was just at. I remember that, and now I'm twenty-four."

He smiled. "Same age as me."

She managed a weak smile in an effort to be nice.

"He only went to prison a few months before he died, and he died five years ago. The police visited him again because they were re-investigating it and that's when he told them he did it. You see, the man was run over many years ago and the police didn't find anyone who had done it. Years later they were looking at it again and they came around asking questions of Abner. That's when he said he did it."

She'd never heard of anyone admitting to an unsolved crime years later. "It all sounds very odd. He just volunteered that he did it? Was there an interrogation, witnesses who came forward or anything?"

"Yes and no." He smiled at her.

She shook her head.

"Yes, he admitted it, and no, there was no interrogation or witnesses who came forward."

She slumped lower in the buggy seat. "The man was run over by a buggy? That doesn't make sense. I can understand how it might cause serious injuries, but death? How fast was the buggy going? I've never heard of a horse and buggy galloping."

"No, a car. Abner claimed he borrowed a car and wouldn't say who from or anything."

"Hmm, that's odd that he would drive a car. He was still in the community, right?"

"Of course. He never left."

She still had some friends on the force from her brief career in law enforcement. They weren't allowed to give out information to civilians, so she'd be asking a lot if she reached out to them. "How can I find out more about what happened?"

"I'll tell you all about it. Thirty-something years ago a man who did odd jobs for your grandfather was run down in the street. His name was Wayne Robinson. The driver didn't stop. The man wasn't too popular, and he had a few enemies. Was it an accident and someone didn't stop?"

"I don't know. How would I have any answers?"

He frowned at her. "I'm not finished. Here's the next question. 'Or, did someone kill him on purpose?'"

"Is there anyone around here who might know what actually happened, in some detail? Do you remember who the investigating officers were?"

His grin widened. "No, but I can take you to some very nice Amish people who can tell you more."

She sighed. "Will they be able to help?"

"I think so. They were trying to get Abner out of jail."

She brightened up. That sounded hopeful. If these people thought he hadn't done it, maybe he hadn't. It also sounded odd that Abner would have claimed to be driving a car. From what her mother said, Abner was a man of God, who was always preaching to his daughter to stay on the narrow path. Would this man have strayed? The grandfather she'd been told about wouldn't have.

He added, "I know these two women well."

"Oh, good. Where can I find them?"

"I'll take you to them right now. Unless you'd like to look at the house first?"

She prioritized everything. If Eugene found out about the skeleton in her family's closet, he'd call off the wedding for sure, and then she wouldn't inherit the house for years. "Take me to these people first, please."

"Okay." He pulled the horse back onto the road and then turned the horse and buggy around.

CHAPTER 2

ETTIE CONTINUED HER KNITTING, helping Elsa-May knit small brown squares to be assembled into teddy bears for the hospital. It was all they'd been doing of late and Ettie wanted nothing more than to get out of the house into the fresh air and sunshine to do something exciting. Much to her sister's annoyance, Ettie had positioned her chair to look out the window. Ettie said it was to see the distant hills and to watch the birds as they flew about, but they both knew it was to watch what the neighbors were doing.

The Charmers had been far too quiet over the last few weeks. There'd been no angry Greville at the door reprimanding them about Snowy's imaginary barking and neither had he pushed the fence palings over again to blame it on poor old Snowy. Stacey his wife, had gone from watering her plants in the front yard in the rain, to not watering them at all. They were dying from lack of attention.

That led Ettie to think …. "Elsa-May, have you seen Stacey lately?"

Elsa-May left off her knitting and looked at her with piercing blue eyes from over the top of her glasses. "You know I haven't. You asked me that yesterday, and the day before."

"Ach nee, that's what I feared. He's killed her. She's lying inside dead, and she died alone. It's so sad. It seems they must have no children because no one ever visits them. She's alone day in and day out ... and to die like that." Ettie made tsk tsk sounds while shaking her head.

"Oh, Ettie, you have such an imagination."

"It's possible it's true. I always knew there was something funny about him and she hasn't stolen any of our mail lately, or watered her dying plants."

Elsa-May chuckled. "She might've stolen our mail and we don't know about it. I mean, think about it. How would we know if she had stolen letters from our box?"

"That's right." Ettie placed her knitting in her lap and tapped a bony finger on her chin. "I usually have far more people writing to me. She must've pinched some letters."

"It was a joke, Ettie."

"Do you think we should knock on their door? Or peep in the window?"

Elsa-May sighed. "Have you ever heard the expression, 'Let sleeping dogs lie?'"

"Nee."

"Forget about the Charmers, would you?"

Ettie blew out a deep breath. One day she'd find out what was really going on with them. One day her sister would agree to accompany her while she peeped in the windows, but going by her sister's attitude it wasn't going to be any time soon.

"Oh, we have a visitor." Ettie folded up her boring knitting, stabbing the end of the needles into the fat round ball of wool. She much preferred her fancy-worked samplers to knitting. Knitting was more Elsa-May's pastime.

"Who is it?" Elsa-May asked.

Ettie stared at the buggy through the window. "It looks like Gabriel Yoder."

"He hasn't visited before."

"And he's got an *Englischer* with him. She's a pretty young girl with long straight fair hair. She's wearing jeans and a blouse and high heels." Ettie was pleased to have visitors to break the monotony of the day especially since the Charmers weren't doing anything interesting.

Ettie was first to the door and Elsa-May was close behind her. Gabriel was smiling at them and heading to the door, while the woman was now across the road with her back to them talking on a cell phone.

～

"IF YOU DON'T MIND, Gabriel, I'll make a quick call to my mother before you knock on the door."

"Sure. I'll wait."

She turned away from him with her back to the house. She hit the speed dial and her mother answered. "Mom."

"Have you arrived yet?"

"Yes. I got here a couple of hours ago."

"How's the food at your bed-and-breakfast?"

"I'll find out tomorrow morning." Her mother was obsessed with food. "The room's nice, but I didn't stay there long. Just enough time to book in and …" She shook her head. "Mom, you didn't tell me your father killed someone."

"Oh, that. I didn't want to upset you."

"You knew?"

"I did."

Selena couldn't believe it. "I wish you'd told me. What will I do if Eugene finds out?"

"He'll just have to deal with it."

Selena swallowed hard. Her mother was a fan of Eugene's

15

and he was the only boyfriend of whom Mom had approved. She could only imagine what Eugene would say once he found out about her grandfather. It was the worst thing she could possibly think of and she wished she'd never come there. "You know he wouldn't like this. I just wish you'd told me."

"I didn't think you'd find out about it and I didn't want to upset you. That's all."

"Well, I'm upset now! And I'll be even more upset if Eugene calls off the wedding because of this. If you'd told me earlier, I might've been able to do something about it."

"I'm sorry, dear."

She heard her mother light up a cigarette. "Are you smoking again, Mom?"

"No."

"You are. I heard the lighter. You told me you'd quit."

"My show's coming on soon. I'll have to go shortly." She heard her mother breathe in deeply and then slowly exhale.

"Don't go. I need to talk. There's a man here who said he didn't do it."

"He *didn't* do it."

"He was innocent?"

"Yes. Definitely."

"How do you know he was innocent for sure?"

"He was always so self-righteous. He wouldn't have done anything wrong. It just wasn't in him."

"Do you know how I can prove that?"

"You'd know. You were on the force. You could investigate it and clear his name, and the family's."

Now, her mother was being facetious.

"I wouldn't know where to start. I was only there for a year and they had me doing paperwork. I didn't step a foot out of the station. I'm not a detective. Although, I did have good training, and paperwork gave me an insight—"

"Oh, gotta go. My show's just started."

"No! Wait, Mom."

"Talk soon." Her mother hung up the receiver—loudly—in her ear.

She looked down at her cell, lost for words. Then she spun around to see Gabriel standing in the doorway of the house flanked by a couple of old Amish ladies. She took a deep breath and made her way to them, hoping they'd be able to shed some light on the problem.

Gabriel introduced her to the old ladies. The larger one was Elsa-May, and the smaller one was Ettie. They both looked kind and friendly.

Ettie grabbed her hand. "It's so nice to meet you, Selena. I remember your mother, Kate. How is she?"

"She's fine." *She's addicted to daytime TV, and she's a chain smoker. She rarely leaves the house since Dad died and she leads a boring life.* It was easier just to say she was fine. No one ever really wanted to know how someone was.

Elsa-May said, "Gabriel tells us you want to find out about Abner, is that right?"

"Yes, I heard he confessed to a hit-and-run incident, but Gabriel assures me everyone around here knows he didn't do it."

"No, he didn't." Ettie shook her head. "Let's go inside."

"Thank you." Selena stepped into the house behind Ettie.

"Come through to the kitchen and we'll make you a cup of hot tea," Elsa-May said.

"That would be lovely, thank you," Gabriel said.

"Yes, it would," Selena agreed.

CHAPTER 3

ONCE THEY WERE in the small kitchen, Selena noticed nearly the entire floor area was taken up by the round table and four chairs. Elsa-May filled the kettle with water while Ettie busied herself cutting a cake.

Gabriel said to her, "Don't worry. Ettie and Elsa-May will find out what's really going on."

Ettie sat down placing the sliced cake in the center of the table while Elsa-May, who was finished placing the kettle on the stove, put small plates in front of everyone. "Help yourselves."

Selena listened as Ettie started the conversation about her grandfather. "We were trying to help him, and we went to the jail a few times but he didn't want to help himself."

"Why not?" Selena asked and then noticed Ettie and Elsa-May exchange glances.

"That's okay, Selena wants to know the truth," Gabriel said.

"That's right. I need to know everything. I need to know if he committed a crime or not. If it was a hit-and-run and he did it, what was he doing driving a car? I mean, he wasn't driving a buggy, was he?"

"Supposedly, he was driving a car at the time. That's what he wanted the police to believe," Ettie said.

"What do you think happened, Ettie?" Selena asked.

"You have to remember this was a long time ago. Detective Kelly wasn't working on the original case. No, it was our dear old friend, Ronald Crowley. Crowley didn't get to the bottom of things, and years later, someone else was re-investigating the case."

"Tell Selena what we were told, Ettie."

"It's a long story."

Elsa-May jumped up to make the tea when the kettle whistled. Selena smiled at the old lady. "Can you give me the short version, then?"

"The dead man worked on his fences —"

"His own fences?" Selena feared she was going to get the long version.

"No. The dead man was redoing Abner's fences because the woman next door was always upset over her alpacas."

"And she hasn't changed," Gabriel interjected sporting a big smile. "She thinks people steal her alpacas and that's why she's worried about the fences coming down," he explained to Selena.

"Was he like a part time handyman or something?"

"That's right." Ettie licked her lips. "We think Abner was protecting somebody, but we cannot say who he was protecting."

"Because we don't know," Elsa-May placed the teapot in the middle of the table. "Would anybody like coffee?"

"No thanks, tea's fine," Selena said, feeling like she would not be able to keep anything down. She placed a small piece of cake on her plate just to be polite and decided she'd make an effort to sip some tea. Perhaps the tea would settle her stomach. "Do you think it's got something to do with the woman who owns the alpacas? Might she be the one who ran over the man?"

"We're not sure of that, but we're fairly certain that Abner knew who did it. And he can't tell us because he's dead now." Ettie sighed and bit into a piece of cake. "If only the dead could talk. What secrets they'd tell us."

"But we can piece together the clues and Ettie would've figured it all out given enough time."

Ettie nodded. "And I stopped trying to figure it out when Abner died, you see. There was no point to it anymore. His daughter had moved away and there was no one in his family left."

"He didn't seem to be bothered by sitting in jail, did he, Ettie?"

"No. Nothing bothered Abner. He was always such a pleasant man."

Selena took a small bite of cake and figured she was wasting her time with the ladies. Then her gaze drifted to Gabriel and he gave her a big smile. All she wanted to do was get out of the small house. She felt like the walls were closing in on her. "It's okay. I don't need to find out. I suppose it's too hard after all this time."

Ettie's eyebrows rose and she stared at Gabriel. "I thought that's why you brought her here, Gabriel."

The two old ladies stared at Gabriel, who in turn looked at Selena.

"So did I," he answered.

"I mean, do you think you can help me find out who he was protecting?"

"We already said so," Elsa-May said, with a touch of frustration.

Ettie put her hand over her sister's, and said to Selena,

"Sometimes we don't need to know everything. Perhaps this is one of those times?"

Suddenly a white fluffy dog, its tail wagging happily, streaked into the kitchen and started pawing Selena's leg. "What a dear little dog." His eyes were black and so was his nose and they stood out in contrast against his white fur.

"Elsa-May, you said you'd put him out."

"I did. I must've forgotten to latch the dog door. I'm terribly sorry, Selena. Snowy has such sharp claws."

Selena giggled. "That's okay. I like dogs. That's the perfect name for him."

"I'll have to remember that," Gabriel said.

She looked over at him wondering why he'd say such a strange thing. As soon as the house was in her name, she'd go back to New York City and she'd hope never to see him again.

"Put him out, Elsa-May."

Elsa-May scooped the dog up and took him outside.

"We can help if you want us to, Selena. It's up to you." Ettie brought the teacup to her lips and took a small sip.

"I'm here for a few days. Thank you. I might think about it."

"Yes, good idea. You have a little think on it."

She doubted if the old ladies would be any help at all. After they had finished their cake and tea, she thanked the ladies and then she and Gabriel left.

As they were about to climb into the buggy, Gabriel said, "You don't trust them?"

"It's not that. I just think they won't be able to help. They were nice ladies and everything, but I've got my own way of doing things."

"And what's that?" he asked.

"I spent a little time on the police force."

"Doing what?"

She stared at him, thinking it was an odd question. Everyone else assumed that police all did the same thing. "I'm a trained police officer, but I didn't stay for long after I met my fiancé."

"Yes that's good. I think a woman really does need to be home all the time."

"What?"

"Your boyfriend didn't want you to work, yes?"

That made her fiancé sound like a chauvinist. "It's not like that."

"My apologies. I didn't mean to offend. The last thing I want is to upset you; it seems that everything I say upsets you."

He was making her head hurt. And he'd just demoted Eugene to her boyfriend rather than her fiancé. Was that deliberate? "Can we just go to my house now?"

"Yes, that's where I'm taking you."

"Are you sure they won't mind us coming by with no notice?"

He shook his head. "They'll be fine."

"Good."

When they pulled up to the house, she was able to have a closer look at the peeling paint. "You said you were using the money for the upkeep." She then looked at him, wondering just how honest he was. "Are you sure you're not keeping the money for yourself?"

He threw his head back and laughed like a maniac. "No. I don't even take anything for my time and sometimes the place takes a lot of my time." He shook his head. "All I'm getting is the happiness of doing something for my dear old friend."

She stared back at the place. It would be quite pretty once

it was painted and maybe had some proper landscaping to set it off. "What would be the value of a place like this?"

"I'd say about one fifty."

"Cents?" she asked while still looking at the shabby exterior.

He laughed again. "Dollars," he said. "Actually, thousand dollars."

"Did you know my grandfather well?" She knew she'd asked him that before, but she found it hard to believe that they could've been friends.

"That's right."

"What was he like?"

"Grumpy sometimes. Well, a lot of the time."

Selena giggled. "That's how I remember him."

"He was a generous man and always lent anyone a hand with anything. A grumpy old man with a good and genuine heart. He was sad—he was alone without his daughter; that's the part of his life that kept him from being cheerful. She meant everything to him after his wife died. I can't say I remember Martha, but she came alive in his stories. I feel like I know her."

"I remember Mom saying she died when Mom was just twelve. That's sad he was alone."

"He had a lot of friends."

"I'm glad."

CHAPTER 4

GABRIEL WENT AHEAD while Selena waited in the buggy. He said a few words to the tenant, Molly, who answered the door. Molly looked past him to Selena and then nodded. Gabriel turned toward Selena and beckoned to her.

Selena hurried over and Gabriel introduced the two women.

"I'm sorry for such short notice, Molly, but I'm in town only for a short time."

"That's fine. Sorry for the mess. Matt, my husband, is at work. He'll be disappointed he didn't meet you."

When she walked into the house, it wasn't a mess. Everything was neat and clean. There were four young children on a rug playing with wooden toys.

"I've got my baby asleep." Molly pointed to the crib and as she did so, Selena noticed she was expecting. The woman would soon have six children and she only looked to be in her early thirties.

"Oh, sorry. I won't speak loudly. Are these all yours?" She pointed to the four children.

"All of them." Molly giggled. "And just speak normally. It wouldn't matter. Not with the noise these four make. He's quite used to sleeping through noise. I want to thank you, Selena, for allowing us to stay here. We would've had nowhere to live if it hadn't been for your kindness."

Selena opened her mouth not knowing what to say. "You're welcome," was all she could think of. She hadn't known of their existence until earlier that day. When she glanced up at Gabriel, he smiled.

"I'll show you through the bedrooms," Molly said. "Or do you want to show Selena around, Gabriel?"

"No, you go ahead."

There were three bedrooms, one small bathroom and another working toilet in a small room outside. Gabriel explained the bathroom had been built on, and when the house was originally built, there had been no bathroom inside.

Selena shook her head. "I don't know how anybody could live like that."

"Everybody did back then, and not just us Amish folk," Gabriel said.

"I guess that's true," she said.

"I'll show you the outside facilities when we finish in here," he said.

Selena shook her head. "You don't need to."

He remained silent and then she was shown the kitchen. Her mother had told her that was the most important room in an Amish household. It was where they cooked and ate, where they canned and preserved their food, and sometimes there were two rooms used as kitchens. In Abner's house, there was one large kitchen. It had a surprisingly lovely view of the countryside. The whole house was a pleasant surprise.

"It's a lovely kitchen. I was here when I was about eight,

but everything looks so different. Thanks for showing me through."

"Of course. Why wouldn't I? I guess you might be thinking about selling. If you do, we'll go to Matt's aunt's place. She has room in her house now that her children have moved out. We won't be out on the street. Don't worry."

Gabriel said, "We'll give plenty of notice if Selena decides to sell."

"Yes, we will. Thank you for showing us through."

"Come back any time. Would you like some coffee before you go?"

Selena smiled at her. "Oh, no thank you."

Gabriel and Selena headed out of the house.

"Are you sure you don't want to see the barn?" Gabriel asked.

"Sure, okay. Oh, is that what you meant by the outside facilities?"

"Yes. What did you think?"

She couldn't keep the smile from her face. "The outside toilet." They both laughed.

"There wouldn't be much to see, but I'll show you that too if you'd really like to see it."

"Just the barn will be enough."

He nodded to the barn. "Come with me." He opened one of the double doors of the barn and light shone through. There were stalls to one side and old buggies, and parts of buggies.

"Oh my, this really does need a cleaning out."

"It does. I'll organize it soon, don't worry. You should've seen it a year ago. I've been gradually getting it cleared."

"I don't remember the barn from when I was here as a kid."

"Your grandfather liked to make things over, and that's

why there's so much stuff in here. He collected bits and pieces from all over the place."

She stepped back. "Okay. I've seen enough."

When they were outside, he closed the door and pulled the metal latch over.

"I'm sorry I was so rude to you when I first arrived. I can see you really have done a good job looking after the place."

"I do have a bank account for it. The rent goes in and then I pay necessities out of it. I'll show you the balance if you'd like. I don't take a cent for myself."

"I'm sure everything's in order, and you're entitled to a management fee. I'll work something out."

"No. I don't want money. I agreed with Abner I'd do it. He didn't expect to pay me and neither did I expect to be paid."

He seemed offended she'd offered to pay him. "My grandfather obviously left you to look after the house for a reason. He trusted you and that's good enough for me. I'm grateful." Halfway back to the buggy, she said, "Do you mind if I just make a quick call to my fiancé before we leave?"

"Go right ahead." He walked a few steps, and then said over his shoulder, "I'll be waiting in the buggy."

"Sure." She was excited about the house and hoped Eugene would be too.

He answered the phone with hurried words. "Yes? Quick."

She hesitated, not happy with his dismissive attitude. It was even more noticeable to her after spending time with Gabriel. Eugene had to have known it was she because he had her name and phone number programmed into his phone. He certainly wouldn't talk to anyone else like that. "It's okay I'll talk to you later."

"No, talk now. You called so there must be a good reason."

"I've just looked through the house."

"Tell me about it tonight. I'll call you." And just like that, he ended the conversation without so much as a 'goodbye,' an 'I love you,' or a 'see you later.'

Even though she was hurt, she fixed a smile on her face, and turned back toward the buggy and her waiting admirer, who was growing on her in a small way.

CHAPTER 5

"Ettie, why didn't you tell Selena that Abner was protecting his daughter?"

Ettie passed the plates to Elsa-May for the washing up after their visitors had left. "Why didn't *you?*"

"Only because *you* didn't."

Ettie sighed. "How could I tell the young lady her mother borrowed or possibly stole a car from somewhere and drove over her old *Englischer* boyfriend and is essentially a murderess?"

Elsa-May placed the plates carefully on the sink and then adjusted her glasses. "I believe the correct usage for that word these days is murderer."

"What does it matter? It means the same thing, so why would I tell Selena that?"

"It's definitely not the same thing. You can't call a man a murderess. Anyway, we'll shelve that word discussion for another time."

"*Denke, Gott,* for that mercy," Ettie prayed under her breath.

"Selena wants to know the truth," Elsa-May said.

"Does she?" Ettie drew her lips together tightly. "Which would she prefer to believe, her mother killed someone, or the killing in cold blood was acted out by the grandfather she barely knew?"

"I see your point of view, Ettie, but there's no escaping that the truth is the truth."

"Correct. I'm not disputing that. I'm just saying, what does it really matter? The man is dead, and Abner's dead. And, we shouldn't keep saying that Kate did it because Kate might not have done it. We've assumed this whole time that she's been guilty with zero proof."

"We have the evidence that Abner said he did it and why would he have said that if he wasn't protecting his only child?"

Ettie said, "That's right, but on the other hand, we don't even know if Wayne Robinson was killed deliberately, or was it accidently—by a stranger who was too scared to stop?"

"I suppose you're right. *Jah*, very true. I hadn't thought about there being more possibilities."

"Well, I'm glad you didn't blab to Selena that her mother was a murderess."

Elsa-May shook her head at her sister's insistence on using that word. She looked back at the dishes. "If Kate didn't do it, I'm still positive Abner was convinced she did."

"That's what we can agree upon."

Elsa-May smiled. "At last we agree on something." After she'd filled up the sink with sudsy water, she turned to Ettie. "What would have made Abner think his daughter killed Wayne?"

"Because she obviously had a good enough reason to kill him. We had this conversation five years ago."

Elsa-May said, "Hmm. I know, but we never got to the bottom of things."

"At the time, we decided not to. We didn't know his

granddaughter would be knocking on our door looking for the truth years later. She was off living somewhere with Kate. And Kate never even came back for her father's funeral."

"One good thing came out of our unexpected visitors."

Ettie looked up from wiping the crumbs off the table. "What was that?"

"We've just had an hour and a half where we didn't talk about the Charmers once."

Ettie groaned. "Don't get me started on *them*." To the sound of Elsa-May's chuckles, Ettie walked over to the kitchen window and peeped out at the house next door. From there, she had a good view of the garden and the two windows at the side of the house. But, to which rooms did those windows belong? They'd been in the living room of the house once before, some time ago when they'd visited Stacey, so Ettie knew the one near the front of the house was the living room. The back window must've belonged to one of the bedrooms, she supposed, or maybe a bathroom.

~

WHEN GABRIEL SAW Selena heading to the buggy after calling her fiancé, he jumped down. Then, he tried to help her up into the buggy and she pulled away from him.

"I can manage, thanks." She squirmed out of his way.

"I'm just trying to help."

"Yes, I know you are." She climbed in, sat down and adjusted her blouse.

He hustled around to the driver's seat and jumped in beside her landing with a thud. "What do you think of your house?"

It was time to throw his words back at him. "It's not mine yet, remember? It's not mine until I get married."

"We can marry tomorrow. Then it will be your house sooner." He chuckled at his own joke.

She had to giggle at his silliness. "I have a perfectly good fiancé, Eugene Ryder, and that's who I'll marry, thanks all the same. We're having a large white wedding with five hundred guests. My wedding planner and I have been planning it for six months, so I will have to decline your offer."

"Okay, but if it's all the same to you, I won't give up."

She stared at him to figure out if he was joking. His face told her he was dead serious.

"So. You didn't answer my question yet. What did you think of the house?" he asked once more as he turned the buggy toward the street.

"It was fine. Better than I thought it would be inside. Do you really think it would be worth one hundred and fifty thousand dollars?"

"I do."

She thought about what that would buy back in her home of New York City. Parking spaces sold for more than that. There didn't seem much point to sell; it would make sense to just keep renting. After the cost of the upkeep, it might give her some good pocket money. Even though Eugene was on a good income, she didn't want to be in the position to ask him for money. They hadn't even discussed what their financial arrangements would be after the marriage.

Eugene had been adamant about her going there to see the place, but he could've estimated on the Internet what the place was worth. That led her to worry about his new secretary. He seemed to get a new one every six months, but this one worried her. Elga's name had come up far too many times in conversations. She'd never met Elga like she'd met his other secretaries. She imagined her as some six-foot-tall Nordic beauty with clear skin, bright blue eyes and naturally blonde hair. Of course, she'd be skinny and wear figure-hugging skirts and tight, low-cut stretchy blouses. Selena bit the inside of her mouth. She hated feeling jealousy toward someone she'd never met and Eugene had never once given her grounds to mistrust him—apart from his long working hours.

Despite Selena trying to talk herself around, her mind kept spiralling into negativity. Was Elga the reason Eugene wanted her to stay in Lancaster County for a few days? He also said it would be good for her to get away from the stress of planning the wedding and he was probably right about that. It had been a nice change to think about something other than the wedding and what might and could go wrong on the day. She felt Gabriel looking at her, and she looked over at him to see him smiling—again.

"Are you figuring out what to do with the place when it's yours?" he asked.

"Yes." She looked back at the house they were moving away from. "It certainly needs painting."

"It *is* on the list of things to do."

"I hope it's at the top of that list or I'd be very concerned about the condition of the place."

"I can go over everything with you. How about we do it over dinner tonight?" He took his eyes off the road and smiled at her.

"Or, you could just tell me now."

He frowned and looked back at the road. "It really just needs painting. It's had new plumbing three years ago, and the Kings have painted the inside in lieu of some rent."

"Ah, good."

CHAPTER 6

AFTER COLLECTING her car from Gabriel's house, Selena went back to her bed-and-breakfast. The room was all she needed since it had a bed with the convenience of an en-suite bathroom. When she was booking it, many of the other places she'd looked at on the Internet had shared bathrooms. Selena pulled down the pastel floral bedspread and collapsed onto the bed. It'd been a huge day.

She reached into her bag and pulled out her phone and pressed Eugene's number. He hadn't called her back as he'd said he would, but that often happened.

He answered and before he said hello, he spat out, "Why haven't you been taking any of my calls?"

"My phone hasn't made a sound all day. There were no missed calls from you. I spoke with you not long ago and you said you were too busy to talk."

"Since then I've called about six times."

"I'm sorry. I've been in and out of range for most of the day. The service around these areas is pretty choppy."

"What was the house like?"

"It needs a bit of work outside, but it seems fine inside. The plumbing's been updated about—"

"Good, good."

She knew she had to delay going home, so she could sort her grandfather business out before Eugene learned of it. "I think I'll have to stay a couple more days."

"Take a few days. That's what I already told you. You need to have a break and wind down. You've been high strung and irritable for the past few weeks."

She giggled. "Have I?"

"You sure have."

"Sorry. It's just that the stress of the wedding's getting to me. I wish you could help me with a few of the decisions."

"Do me a favor, would you, and never say anything like that ever again?" He was back to being angry. "That's exactly why I'm paying a fortune for this wedding planner. The bride's parents pay for most weddings like this, but since you've only got your mother and she's got nothing, I'm left to foot the bill. I can't do everything, Selena."

"I'm not asking you to do everything, but I don't think you understand how huge this has become because of all the guests. I don't know any of these people. They're all your guests."

"I admit it's becoming a lot bigger than I planned."

"Well, we can't do anything about it now."

"Selena, I hate getting angry with you, but do you understand I've got to work to make the money to spend on the wedding? If I'm planning the wedding too, it'll take my time from work and if I'm not earning the money there will be no wedding. Do you get it?"

"Yes, I get it, and I understood the first time you told me."

"Good. Now, can you tell me we won't need to have this conversation again?"

"We won't." This was the same disagreement they'd been having for the past several weeks. "How was your day?"

"Same old same old."

"No interesting new cases?"

There was silence and she knew she had said something wrong. Eventually, he said, "Don't you ever listen?"

She hated it when he spoke to her like he was reprimanding a child. "What do you mean?"

"I don't have the time to take on any new cases until I finish with the ones I've got. I've got to go. Another call's coming." He ended the call without saying goodbye.

Selena tossed her phone onto her bed, upset that there had been no lovey-dovey talk, especially since she was so far from home. She wasn't that far geographically, but she might as well have been in another country. He hadn't even told her he loved her or missed her. Was that what it was going to be like when they married?

The romance had disappeared from the relationship right after the engagement announcement. It was as though that was a job done and he'd dusted off his hands afterwards. He'd found a wife and checked that box, and then moved on to the next thing on his life's to-do-list. She put his behavior down to the stresses of his job.

Slumping back into the pillow, she pushed everything out of her mind, closed her eyes and let her mind drift.

SELENA WOKE and looked at the clock. Eleven. In a dopey haze, she first thought she'd slept in to eleven the next day before she realized it was still night. Worry gnawed at her stomach as she sat on the bed. There would be no wedding and certainly no marriage to Eugene if she didn't find out who really had run that man down. There was no other way around things; she had to clear her grandfather's name and find out why he'd confessed to a crime he hadn't had anything to do with.

She really needed the help of a proper trained detective. First thing tomorrow she'd visit the local police station and see what she could find out about the hit-and-run her grandfather had admitted to.

CHAPTER 7

THE FIRST THING Selena did when she woke was make a call to one of her friends to find out who the lead detective was in that area. They texted back that it was Detective Keith Kelly, and she remembered Ettie had mentioned his name.

After a hastily eaten breakfast of omelette and toast in the communal dining room, she went back to her room to finish getting ready for the day. She texted Eugene and was pleased to get a text right back with the words, *I love you,* and there were two red hearts at the end of the words. That immediately put her in a good mood and relaxed her.

SELENA APPROACHED the officer at the front desk and asked to speak to Kelly and to her delight he was in the building and able to see her. She was told to wait for him in the seating area. A few minutes later, a man in a rumpled brown suit with a receding hairline made his way to her.

"Selena Lehman?"

She stood up. "That's right."

He extended his hand. "Detective Kelly."

She shook his hand. "I was hoping I might have a quick word with you."

"Certainly. Come this way."

She followed him down a narrow hallway and into his office. It reminded her of where she used to work.

He sat behind his desk, and as soon as she sat opposite, she said, "I'm here about a hit-and-run that happened quite a few years ago. I'm in town because ... Well, it's a long story why I'm here. I didn't know until I got here that my grandfather had confessed to the crime, but everyone who knew him says they're sure he didn't do it." The words had tumbled out of her mouth and she wondered if he understood any of what she'd just said.

"Was your grandfather convicted of the hit-and-run?"

"He was in jail for it because he confessed to it. I believe ... well, I've been told that he died before it came to court."

"Name?"

"Abner Troyer, and he supposedly ran over a man called Wayne Robinson. Wayne was the victim."

Kelly turned away from her to tap away at the keyboard of his desktop computer. "Ah, yes, here we are; Abner Troyer. He was in jail for contempt of court for twenty days because he refused to swear on the bible in court."

"He wouldn't, because he was Amish. I know they all refuse to do that. Instead they take a solemn affirmation. I think that's what it's called. They never take any oaths, you see."

"Yes, I do know that. He was Amish?"

"That's right."

He looked back at the computer. "Here we go. Seems he also refused to recite anything to say that what he was about to say was the whole truth."

"Oh. Really?"

"Yes. He refused both. He did tell us he did it. He signed a statement. The incident happened nearly twenty-five years ago and he confessed to the crime when it was being re-investigated a few short years ago. I wasn't the detective working on the case, but I do have a vague recollection of my colleagues working on it."

"It's very important that I clear my grandfather's name. Could you reopen the case?"

He scratched behind his ear in an agitated manner. "We don't have the funding to investigate cases we've already re-investigated. One re-investigation plus the original investigation equals two investigations." He leaned back in his chair. "Your grandfather admitted to the crime, and that was the conclusion of our findings, then we handed it over to the court system. Effectively, our job's done and we've washed our hands of it." He raised his hands in the air while giving her a sympathetic smile.

"Your findings were wrong, though. I believe he wasn't guilty."

He nodded. "That's not uncommon. Most relatives find it hard to believe their loved ones are capable of committing crimes. The best thing I can suggest for you is to go home and forget about it."

"I can't do that. I can't do that when everyone is saying he's not guilty. And, quite frankly, don't you think it a little odd that an Amish man was convicted of a crime involving a car?"

"I've had a lot of involvement with the Amish and nothing they do surprises me. People are still people. Passions are raised, tempers flare, and ... so it goes."

"Don't you care that Abner might not have been guilty?" She hadn't wanted to say that, but it appeared he wasn't worried as long as they found someone to be held account-able for the crime, so they could say they'd done their job.

"Not really. Abner confessed, so that's that. No one held a

gun to his head to make him confess. If he didn't do it he wouldn't have said he did."

"After talking to some of his friends, they tell me they're convinced he didn't do it."

A hint of a smile met his lips. "That's normal. No one wants to think of their friends in that way. No one really knows what anyone's capable of when they're pushed, including our loved ones. From the report I just read, the man was known to your grandfather, so it was more than an accidental running-someone-over and covering it up. No, they obviously had some falling out." He slowly nodded. "His friends would say he was innocent; that's what friends do." A smile creased Kelly's lips.

"Look, this is very important to me. Do I have to hire a private detective or something to get to the bottom of things?"

He leaned back in his chair and crossed his arms over his chest. "Why does this mean so much to you, Ms. Lehman?"

She swallowed hard. "I'm about to get married and my fiancé is a lawyer and if he found out about my grandfather, it wouldn't be good. It came as a huge shock to me, I can tell you that. I only recently learned of it." When Kelly just stared at her, she jumped to her feet. "I can see that I'll have to find out what really happened for myself."

"You're entitled to do that as long as you don't break any laws along the way."

"I was on the force briefly."

His eyebrows rose slightly. "Very good—so you know the boundaries in this kind of thing?"

"Yes, I do. At least I have some help." She was about to walk out the door.

He stood up. "You have help already?"

She turned around. "I have a couple of old ladies who say

that they know you. They thought you'd help me, but I'll have to tell them they were wrong."

He chuckled. "Would that be Mrs. Smith and Mrs. Lutz?"

She shrugged her shoulders. "I only know their first names, Ettie and Elsa-May."

"That's them. See what they can come up with. If there's anything there they'll get to the bottom of it."

She wanted to say, *thanks for nothing*, but she held her tongue in case she needed his help in the future. "Goodbye, Detective Kelly."

"I will look into things when I have a spare moment."

She regretted her harsh tone. "Would you?"

"I will. I give you my word on it."

"Thank you. Thank you so much. I'd really appreciate it. I'm staying at the—"

"Leave your details at the desk. They'll email them through to me."

"Sure. Thank you again." She headed out the door feeling she was making some small progress and she was also pleased that the detective knew of the two old ladies. He hadn't even said one negative thing about them.

After she'd left her details with the officer at the front desk, she walked down the steps of the police station wondering how to get back to Ettie and Elsa-May's house. She couldn't wait to get started on the investigations and she'd apologize to them if she had seemed weird yesterday.

She headed out on the road to where she thought Ettie's house was but she came to a dead end.

She went back to the bed-and-breakfast and took a left. She was certain that was the way. She drove on and on for miles and there was nothing but countryside. Ettie and Elsa-May lived in a neighborhood with a small group of quaint houses.

Soon she came upon an Amish man plowing a field with

two horses pulling the plow. The man looked so at peace with nature as he sat in solitude under his large straw hat. He noticed her and gave her a wave. She smiled and gave a wave back.

After driving another few miles, she knew from the vast open countryside she'd gone in the wrong direction. She was just about to turn around when she drove over a small rise and saw a village up ahead. Before she got there, roadside stalls came into view. Amish people were gathered behind the stalls.

"They might know where these old ladies live," she murmured to herself before she stopped the car. She got out and made her way over.

"Are you looking for some good vegetables, miss? We have turnips and pumpkin. Lovely in soup."

She couldn't help smiling at the young boy with his wide grin that was missing one of his front teeth. He would've been only about six. "No thank you. I might have a few of those lovely looking apples."

"I'll get you a bag and you can fill it."

"Thank you."

The boy rushed away and came back with a paper bag.

"That's kind of you." She noticed someone who might have been his mother sitting on a chair behind the stall, not too close, but close enough to speak with. As she filled the bag, she said, "Excuse me, would you know a couple of Amish ladies called Ettie and Elsa-May?"

"Yes." The lady stood and came closer.

"I'm looking for their house, but I've lost my way."

The young woman smiled. "They're nowhere around here. You go back the way you came about five miles, then take a left just after the bridge—"

"Excuse me, but do you know their address? It'll be easier for me if I just get that. I can put it into my GPS."

"No, I don't know their address, but I know how to get there. I'll tell you, it's simple. You go back the way you came for about five miles, then take a left just after the bridge; the road splits into two and then you take the left fork, followed by the very next right. Follow the road up the rise and their road is just left, no, I mean right after the shanty. You can't miss it." The woman smiled at her.

Selena nodded and wondered why even the Amish said, 'you can't miss it,' after they gave complicated directions. "Thanks." All she remembered was, *go back five miles and take the left after the bridge.* She said to the cute little boy, "I've got eight apples. How much will that be?"

"Two dollars, thanks, miss."

She opened her coin purse and gave him five dollars. "There's a little extra something."

"That's too much," he said with his face screwed up.

"Keep the change."

The boy's face beamed and he looked back at his mother to get her approval. She gave him a small nod and thanked Selena.

Selena headed back to her car with her bag of apples, feeling good from her encounter with the Amish people. She didn't even particularly like apples, but she had to buy something from them. Instead of risking getting lost again, she headed back into town and found her bed-and-breakfast. From there, she'd go to Gabriel's house and get Ettie and Elsa-May's address.

CHAPTER 8

SHE PULLED up at Gabriel's house hoping he'd be more normal today. She took a deep breath and knocked on his door. He opened it with a big smile plastered over his face. "Selena."

"Hello, Gabriel."

He stepped outside onto the porch and looked her up and down. As he did so he said, "You're looking lovely today. Very nice. You look much more relaxed than you did yesterday."

"Thank you. I'm wondering if you might be able to give me Ettie and Elsa-May's address?"

"Why's that?"

"Because I'm going to ask them if they can help me find out the truth about this hit-and-run business. I need to clear my grandfather's name."

"Yes, yes, and I don't blame you at all. If it were my grandfather, I would want to clear his name also."

"Thank you. What's their address?"

"Why don't I drive you?"

"No, that's not necessary."

He placed his hand over his heart. "Sincerely, I would love to drive you there and be involved in helping you with your grandfather, who was also my very good friend. I really want to help in any way I can. Please don't deny me that. Don't leave me out of this."

She looked at the sincerity in his dark eyes and she couldn't deny him what he asked. "Okay. Yes, I guess that would be okay, but I think we should go in my car today."

"My horse could do with the exercise, if you don't mind."

If she insisted on going in her car, she would be denying his horse exercise. He was very clever the way he worded things. She wondered if he was aware of what he was doing. She smiled back and nodded. "Okay. We'll go in the buggy."

"Excellent. You might want to wait here and I'll get it hitched."

"Okay."

WHEN SHE CLIMBED up into the buggy beside him, she said, "I really didn't think I'd be doing this again today."

"Doing what? Visiting the ladies?"

"No, going in a horse-drawn buggy again for the second day in a row."

He laughed. "Why not?"

"It was fine for a one time thing. It is very slow compared to a car."

"We don't need to get anywhere fast."

"By we, do you mean the Amish in general?"

"Yes. You'll get used to it and learn to love it." He looked across at her and smiled.

She thought it best not to say anything to him. There were too many other things on her mind. This man's infatuation with her was the least of her problems. "I tried to find them myself, but ended up lost. I came across some Amish people selling things by the side of the road and they gave me directions, but I'm afraid I'm directionally challenged. I can't live without a GPS."

"I've wondered a lot when I was younger what it would be like to drive a car. I don't think it would be as good as a buggy."

"Let's just say it's different. Way different."

AFTER WAITING for Gabriel to secure the buggy outside Ettie and Elsa-May's house she walked with him up to the front door. Gabriel leaned forward and knocked. When Ettie opened the door, Gabriel said, "Surprise." Elsa-May then peered over the top of Ettie's shoulder.

Ettie smiled at Selena, looking pleased to see her. "We were just talking about you and your grandfather."

"I've come here today to ask you if you would help me find out the truth of what happened. It's very important to me that my grandfather's name is cleared."

"We'd love to help, wouldn't we, Elsa-May?"

"We would. I don't know why we stopped looking into it."

"We stopped because he died," Ettie said with a frown aimed at her sister.

"I know that, Ettie." Elsa-May frowned at her sister. "Well, come inside and we'll figure out a plan of action."

"Thank you," Selena said as the two ladies stepped aside.

"I'm coming too, as the driver." Gabriel gave a laugh.

"That's a very important job." Elsa-May patted him on his back and then guided him into the living room.

ONCE THEY WERE SEATED, Snowy jumped all over the visitors.

Elsa-May scolded him and ordered him back in his dog bed. "Now you stay there. Shame on you." She shook a finger at him and Snowy looked at her with big round eyes and then settled himself down with his head between his front paws. She looked back at Gabriel and Selena. "Sorry about that."

"It doesn't bother me," Gabriel said.

"Or me. He's fine," Selena added.

Ettie said, "Sit down, Elsa-May, so we can talk"

"I was just about to. I had to put Snowy in his bed; if I had wings I'd be quicker, but I don't. Be patient."

Ettie sat still with her hands in her lap until Elsa-May sat back down. "Now, I think the first person we should speak with should be Patricia. She owns the alpacas next door to Abner's house."

"Should we talk with Wayne Robinson's relatives or friends?" asked Selena.

"In time. Firstly, I want to see what Patricia has to say because she made a huge fuss about being angry with Wayne."

"Yes, that's right. Abner told me that she thought Wayne was stealing the alpacas," Gabriel said.

Ettie nodded. "We'll talk to all the people we talked with before and see if they say anything different. Then we'll branch out talking to people we have never spoken with before. How does that sound?"

"Very good. Everything would be much faster in the car, but Gabriel insists on going in the buggy."

Gabriel stared at Selena. "There's nothing better than riding in a buggy on a beautiful day such as today."

Selena turned her head and looked out the small window at the cold sky. "It's not such a beautiful day for this time of year. The sky is gray and cloudy."

"Every day you wake up alive is a good day to me." Elsa-May chuckled.

Gabriel threw his head back and laughed.

"Shall we go then?" Selena asked.

"She's anxious to get started," Gabriel told them.

"Yes. We'll go. You two go on ahead and we'll be out in a minute. We just need to get ready."

CHAPTER 9

SELENA SAT in the backseat of the buggy and watched the old ladies come out in their black coats and black over-bonnets.

Elsa-May decided to sit in the front and Ettie sat in the back with Selena. They traveled down miles of winding roads until they came to the lane that led to Abner's house. Just when they reached the house, it started to rain lightly.

"Ah look, alpacas, Elsa-May."

Elsa-May frowned at her sister. "It *is* an alpaca farm, Ettie."

"I know that, but how many of them does she have?"

"I'm not sure, but she rotates the paddocks, and it looks like they're all in the front this time," Gabriel said. "And that's your house there." Gabriel pointed at Selena's house.

"Yes, I know," Selena said.

"We'll have to leave the buggy here and go the rest of the way on foot."

Selena looked at the large and differing signs on the gate warning people not to go in. There were six of them, all hand drawn and all looking as though they were of varying ages.

No ENTRY, this means you.
   Do not Enter under any circumstances.
   This farm is not a tourist attraction.
   Absolutely No Trespassing.
   Private Property.
   Trespassers will be prosecuted.

"UM, perhaps we shouldn't go in," Selena said.

Ettie shook her head. "She knows us. She's talked to us before."

"That was years ago, Ettie. She wouldn't remember us."

"Is she Amish?" Selena asked.

"No," Elsa-May said.

The ever-happy Gabriel said, "It's okay. She knows me. She'll be okay, and it's stopped raining. Come along." He slipped through the wire fence at the side of the gates and held the wires apart for the ladies to slip through.

Selena was grateful the rain was holding off, and she helped Elsa-May keep her balance and stopped her dress from being snagged on the edge of the fence.

"Thank you, Selena," Elsa-May said as she straightened herself up.

Ettie got through without a problem. "Let's go."

They all followed Gabriel up the slight hill that led to the house. Paddocks of alpacas, that were very interested in them, flanked the road. Gabriel walked right up and knocked on the door while the three women stood behind him.

When the door of the house opened, a woman of around seventy stood there. Under one arm she held a large rifle. A black hat was pulled low over her face, and she wore faded jeans, big boots, and a red and black checkered shirt. If it weren't for her small and delicate features, she might have been mistaken for a man.

"Hello, Mrs. Langerfield. It's lovely to see you again," Gabriel said.

"Can't you read?"

"Don't you remember me? I talked to you a couple of months ago."

"Who are you? I'm not a tourist attraction. Didn't you see the *Do not Enter Under Any Circumstances* sign at the front gate?"

Gabriel continued, "I did, but I didn't think it applied to me."

"Well, it did. I don't like to be disturbed and neither do my animals."

He ignored her protests and kept talking, a little faster than before. "I'm the caretaker of Abner's house next door. Don't you remember me? We talked about the weather just two weeks ago, and you said you were pleased with the fences."

She stared at him. "That's right. I'm glad that man who stole my alpacas is finally gone. I haven't had one gone missing since."

"I've made sure the fences are well maintained even though we both have that responsibility. We just have a couple of quick questions. This young lady here is Abner's granddaughter."

Selena stepped forward. Patricia looked at Selena and nodded. Gabriel then introduced everybody to Patricia.

Ettie said, "We have already met. We met a few years ago when I was asking you questions about Abner and the man who was run down years ago. Do you remember?"

She shrugged her shoulders. "If you want to ask me something make it quick."

"Do you remember a man, Wayne Robinson, who used to work on the farm helping Abner?"

"He was the one run over, wasn't he?"

"That's the one."

"I remember him well. I just mentioned him. He stole my animals."

Selena asked, "Do you know anyone who would have wished him harm?"

She narrowed her eyes and shifted her gaze from one person to the other. "What's this all about?"

"My grandfather admitted to running over Wayne, but I don't think he did it and I've learned they were on friendly terms."

"That's right. He admitted to doing it, so is that not enough for you? What's it got to do with me?"

"We don't believe he did it," Elsa-May said.

"What did you know about Wayne?" Ettie asked.

"Nothing, but I reckon he was stealing my alpacas, and that's all. That's as much as I know. He had shifty eyes. The fences were always down and one by one they went missing."

"How many did you lose?" Selena asked.

"Three."

"Did you call the police?"

"I like to settle things myself."

"How would you do that?" Selena asked.

"I didn't have to. He got killed. Those animals were my pets and the rest of the herd missed them. I told Abner about it, but he wouldn't believe the man was stealing them. If Abner had told him to stay off his land, none of this would ever have happened. From the time that Wayne man came onto Abner's land, I knew he was trouble."

"Was he here a lot?" Selena asked.

"He helped Abner about the place and that's all I can tell you. It's too far back and the old memory's not as good as it used to be. Whenever something needed doing, he was the one Abner called. I thought it unusual because he wasn't one of you people." She nodded at Gabriel. "You Amish stick together, don't you?"

"Yes, and normally we help each other. Perhaps this man needed money and Abner was helping him out."

"Huh. Exactly and he was helping himself to my alpacas along the way." The woman hitched her gun up higher on her hip. "I'm sorry I can't help you more than that. Make sure you latch the gate on your way out."

"We came through the fence," Gabriel said.

She shook her head. "I hope you didn't loosen the wires."

"No, I don't think we did. We appreciate your help on this. Thank you very much." Before Gabriel had finished thanking her, she'd closed the door on them.

They headed back to the buggy.

"She was no help at all," Elsa-May said.

"Where to now?" Selena asked Ettie.

"Right now, I'm a bit peckish." Ettie knew she would have to drag the day out, in the hope Selena would give up and go back home.

Selena glanced at her wristwatch. "It's only eleven."

"We have lunch early around these parts," Elsa-May said.

"You'll feel better once you've had something to eat," Gabriel told her.

She had no choice but to agree since it was three against one. "I guess we could grab something to eat, but it won't take long, will it?"

Gabriel said, "I'll take us to the nearest diner."

Begrudgingly, Selena agreed.

CHAPTER 10

THE FOUR OF them ordered hamburgers. At first Selena was a little frustrated that the other three had ordered menu items that needed to be cooked rather than something quicker. Then she decided to enjoy the experience of going to a diner. She was so used to going to fancy restaurants and eating gourmet food when all she ever wanted was to sink her teeth into a burger with the works. At the kind of restaurants Eugene liked, she felt their serving portions were far too small and were more of a snack rather than a meal.

While they waited for their food to be brought to their booth in the back of the diner, Selena asked, "Who was the man who was killed? We need to find out all about his life. That's what we need to do."

Gabriel asked, "Couldn't you find out from your police friends?" He said to the older ladies, "Selena was a year in the police force."

"Really?" Ettie asked.

"That would've been interesting," Elsa-May said.

Selena pushed a couple of strands of her hair off her face. "Not as interesting as it sounds. I was stuck in an office or at the front desk. Anyway, to answer your question, Gabriel, I haven't asked them because I don't want to compromise their positions. We need to find out if there were witnesses to the crime and about the car that was driven, that kind of thing."

"I can answer that," said Ettie. "There were no witnesses, because it was late at night. The police never knew what kind of car they were looking for, which made things hard for them."

"Well, we need to know who Wayne's friends were and what was happening in his life at the time. Did someone murder him? That's what I'm getting at. Maybe it wasn't just a random hit-and-run and Abner knew who did it."

"You could be right, but I think we should follow my leads first," Ettie said. "I'm doing it methodically by going over old ground before we approach the new." Ettie stared at her without blinking and Selena didn't dare disagree.

"She's always been right about these things," Elsa-May said.

Selena looked at Elsa-May and nodded. "Okay. It won't hurt to talk to a few more people, I guess. It's possible my grandfather was protecting someone. But if that's the case, it still leaves the mystery of who it was and why. Was he protecting a murderer, or was he protecting someone who accidently ran over the person and fled the scene, possibly because they were scared?"

"That would be a normal reaction," Gabriel said. "Is that still a crime?"

"Of course," Selena said.

"But would Abner have known which one of those you just mentioned might have been true? A deliberate act or an accident? If he learned someone close to him had done it he still might not have known."

Selena nodded. "I guess that's true. If Abner didn't do it, and we can rule out police intimidation, why else would he confess?" Everyone looked at her blankly apart from Gabriel who kept smiling at her. "It's not unheard of that innocent people confess to crimes. There are many reasons for that to happen. Who else is on your list, Ettie?" Selena asked.

"The brother, Terrence Robinson, is the next person."

"Oh good. Someone close to Wayne. And what do we hope to find out from the brother?"

"Anything we can."

"Have you talked to him in the past?"

Ettie nodded. "We did when Abner was in jail."

At that moment, their four hamburgers arrived. Even though Selena hadn't thought she was hungry, her mouth began watering at the sight of them.

~

WHEN THEY HAD FINISHED their lunch, Ettie opened up her book and gave Gabriel the address of Terrence Robinson, Wayne's brother. Then they were on their way.

This time Ettie knocked on the door and she was pleased when Terrence opened it. He was a pleasant looking man in his early forties. Ettie's gaze was drawn to his foot that was in a large plaster cast; he was leaning on crutches. He smiled and greeted them when she reminded him of who she was. Then when she told him why they were there, he invited them inside.

"You're lucky to find me home. I'm on sick leave because of this leg." He nodded to it. "I get around on crutches all right but can't do construction like this. Anyway, take a seat."

"Thank you," Ettie said as everyone sat in the living room. "A few years ago, I asked you a few questions when my friend, Abner Troyer, was imprisoned for running over your brother."

"I remember."

"He didn't do it," Gabriel said.

"I do doubt it was the Amish man, even though he confessed. He must've been confused or something." He shook his head. "I warned him he was playing a dangerous game. Wayne, I mean. My brother was involved with women all over the place. He was a playboy. He was seeing two of your kind."

"Two Amish women?" Elsa-May asked.

He nodded.

"You know the names?" Gabriel asked.

"No."

"Was there anybody who might have wanted him out of the way?" Selena asked.

"Only about sixty women, and maybe some of their husbands." He shook his head. "My guess is that one of them finally did him in."

"Had there been attempts on his life before?" Selena asked.

He looked across at Selena. "Not to my knowledge. And you're Abner Troyer's granddaughter?"

"That's right and I'm trying to clear his name."

"Well, I wish you all the luck in the world, but I'm afraid I can't help you."

"If you do remember anything, can you call me on this number?" Selena leaned forward with a slip of paper.

"Certainly. Wait a minute. I do remember a man who was furious with him."

"Who was it?" Selena asked.

"An Amish man he was having trouble with."

Gabriel said, "Not Abner?"

"No not him. A younger man. He kept telling him to stay away from his girlfriend and …" He shrugged his shoulders. "And that's all I know."

"You don't remember the name or what he looked like?" Elsa-May asked.

"No because I only remember my brother telling me about it and that's all."

"Thank you for your help," Elsa-May said.

"It's awful he went that way, but he wouldn't listen to any of us."

"Any of us?" Ettie asked.

"Yes, my sister and I."

"Ah yes, Jill James. We have her on the list to speak with next."

"Did he have any friends we can speak to?" Selena asked.

He shook his head. "He didn't have friends, really. He had plenty of girlfriends."

"Well, thank you for your time," Ettie said pushing herself to her feet. "No need to get up. We'll close the door behind us."

"Okay, thanks."

CHAPTER 11

WHEN THEY WERE all seated in the buggy, Selena pulled out her cell phone and started tapping on it.

"What are you doing?" Ettie asked.

"I'm making notes in my iPhone, so I don't forget anything."

"Why don't you use a book and a pen?"

She laughed. "I don't know. I'm just used to using this. I can also email it to myself when I'm done and I won't lose it like I could lose a book."

"You might lose it if you don't always put it in the same place when you finish with it."

Selena smiled at Ettie. "Thanks for the tip. What next?"

"Next on this list is the sister, Jill James. She and Wayne lived in the same house until Jill kicked him out and kept the dog. You see, both wanted the same dog." Ettie looked down at her notes. "At least, I think that's what my notes say."

"You think the sister killed him for the dog?" Selena asked.

"No, although some would kill over a pet, but that wasn't the case here, I don't think. If the sister killed him it might not have been over a dog; it's often not about any one thing when someone gets murdered. It can be something small and that adds with all the other annoying things that the person's ever done until the potential killer can't take it anymore."

"It sounds like you've had experience?"

"With people who irritate me?" Ettie asked, giving Elsa-May a sideways glance.

Selena shook her head. "No, with murderers."

"Unfortunately, I have."

"I'd like to hear about it, but another day. How far to Jill's place?"

"I think an early night's in order," Elsa-May said.

Selena stared at Elsa-May. "Night? It's only early afternoon."

"Yes, we can start again tomorrow," Ettie said. "We'll go to Jill's first."

Selena held her head in her hands. With the slowness of the buggy and the unhurried pace of these elderly ladies, she felt she was going nowhere—fast. "Can I have a look at your notes, Ettie?" Things would be much more efficient if she investigated by herself.

Ettie hugged the book to herself. "It wouldn't help. My writing's too bad for anyone else to read."

"I could try."

"No!" Elsa-May turned around from the front seat. "You don't want to look at her messy handwriting. There's nothing in there anyway."

"Elsa-May's right. Just a list of possible people for us to visit again. Like Jill James."

"Okay. We'll speak with her tomorrow, then?"

Ettie nodded still hugging the book to her chest. "Yes. First thing tomorrow."

Selena had to agree.

"I can drive us tomorrow, too, if you'd like," Gabriel suggested.

Elsa-May patted him on his shoulder. "Thank you, Gabriel."

"No," Selena said. "It would be much faster if I drove the car."

"We don't like the cars," Ettie said.

"But I thought you could ride in cars, just that you couldn't own them or be the one behind the wheel."

Elsa-May frowned at her. "That's right, but why would we go in a car when we can travel in this lovely buggy of Gabriel's? Where is Jill's place, Ettie?"

Ettie opened her book. "It's not too far. Close enough for the buggy. At least, it was where she was living last time we visited her. She might have moved, but her brother didn't mention she had."

"All we can do is knock on the door," Elsa-May said. "Tomorrow, I meant."

Selena nodded. "I'd like to talk with the sister since his brother didn't seem to know too much about Wayne's life."

Ettie stared at the passing scenery with the book clutched close to her. She'd have to leave it home tomorrow. She couldn't risk Selena looking in it because of what it said about Kate, Selena's mother.

When Ettie and Elsa-May got home, they stood on their porch waving at Gabriel's buggy as it left.

"Elsa-May, we're going to have to go back to the brother and see what he says without Selena being there. I'm certain he knows more than he's letting on."

"Okay. When will we do that?"

"Maybe this afternoon, or maybe tomorrow."

Elsa-May nodded. "How about now?"

"Are you up to it?"

"Sure." Elsa-May smiled.

"What about all that 'early night' business?"

"I was just delaying things, like you were with the long lunch."

Ettie nodded. "Good idea."

THEY CALLED a taxi and arrived back at Terrence's house.

He opened the door surprised to see them there. "Oh, you're back."

Elsa-May said, "I hope you don't mind, but we came back without Abner's granddaughter."

"Well, come in." He adjusted the crutches under his arms and took a step back.

"We're sorry to have you hobble to the door again," Elsa-May said as she walked in ahead of Ettie.

He chuckled. "That's okay. I'm not supposed to sit around all day."

Once they were in the lounge room, Ettie said, "We want to get to the bottom of things about this accident with your brother. We thought you might not have been able to talk freely in front of Selena."

He nodded. "That's right I didn't tell you that the world would be a better place if he wasn't around." He chuckled again. "But seriously, I didn't know if she knew about her mother's relationship with Wayne, so I kept quiet about it. Apart from throwing out a hint."

That was something Ettie didn't know, but had often wondered.

Elsa-May's eyes grew wide. "Did you tell us that last time?"

"Probably not. The secret doesn't seem to matter so much now. It was forbidden on her part of course, since he wasn't Amish like she was."

"So as far as you were aware, Kate Troyer was definitely having a relationship with Wayne?" Ettie asked.

"That's right."

"And how did it end?"

He shook his head. "Another dreadful ding dong fight. They always had dreadful fights. I know because I used to live with Jill and Wayne. I moved out and Wayne and Jill were left."

"How bad were the fights?"

"Nothing physical just a lot of screaming. Now, since I've told you that, I might as well tell you something else. I know that Wayne was blackmailing someone."

Ettie and Elsa-May looked at each other. That was something they'd never heard.

"Who?" Ettie asked.

"A man, that's all I know."

"And that was the man who, you told us, was furious with Wayne?"

"That's right. I was throwing you out a hint."

"Another one? Hmm. Thank you."

He shrugged his shoulders. "That's all I know."

"We appreciate that. Is there anything else you haven't told us?" Elsa-May asked.

He scratched his nose. "That's it."

"What about alpacas?" Elsa-May asked.

Ettie stared at her sister wondering why she was asking. She must've believed Patricia had her animals go missing.

Terrence chuckled. "Are you talking about Pat?"

"Patricia Langerfield."

"That's the one. She's our cousin. Wayne and she never got along. It went way back. She accused him of stealing her alpacas, and she accused him of cutting the brake lines to her car."

Ettie and Elsa-May stared at one another and then Ettie

asked, "How are you related? She was talking to us like she barely knew Wayne."

"Our fathers were brothers. There was an inheritance from my grandfather and it went to Patricia's side of the family. Wayne never got over it."

"And he harassed her?"

He nodded. "He called it 'harmless fun.'"

Ettie and Elsa-May soon left when they figured they'd found out everything from him.

CHAPTER 12

AN HOUR LATER, Ettie and Elsa-May were seated in front of Detective Kelly in his office.

"I know why you're here. You're trying to prove a friend of yours wasn't guilty of a hit-and-run incident."

"That's right," Ettie said while Elsa-May nodded.

Kelly leaned back. "As I said to the young lady when she came to ask me to look into it—"

"She came here?"

"Yes. I had a young woman here early this morning, by the name of Selena Troyer."

"And have you?" Ettie asked.

He frowned at Ettie. "Have I what?"

"Looked into it?"

"Not yet. I haven't had a spare moment. You've managed to catch me between appointments, so it was good timing on your part."

"Ettie and I were wondering if there's anything in the file about Wayne Robinson, the man who died, having a relationship with two Amish women, or even one?"

Ettie added, "Because we're fairly certain Abner's

daughter was having a relationship with Wayne. And we think that's why Abner took the blame."

"To protect the daughter?" he asked.

Both ladies nodded.

He pulled a face. "Why is this all being dredged up now?"

"Selena wants to clear his name."

"Very well, I'll see what I can do. I might have some time later this afternoon." He looked from one sister to the other and breathed out heavily. "Okay, I'll have a quick look now."

Ettie smiled. "Would you?"

"Yes. I'd like to get to the bottom of things too, if it'll keep you both out of my hair. I don't have much of it left." Kelly chuckled.

Ettie looked at his hair, and saw that he was right about that.

Kelly then turned to one side and angled the screen of his desktop computer toward himself. He took a moment and then tapped and paused to read what was on the screen.

"Looks as though he was hit from behind while he walked a lonely stretch of road. Says here he had been at a bar, and a lady friend took him home. She noticed he didn't go inside, but walked away from the house. Now, I'm just looking at the autopsy paperwork. He had abrasions on him, and he appeared to have rolled down the slight embankment to the side of the road, all consistent with being hit by a motor vehicle. His shoes were found yards away. His socks and shoes had been literally knocked off him."

"Amazing." Elsa-May shook her head.

"It's common in these kind of impacts. From the evidence at the scene, it appears he was walking on the side of the road, not close to the edge and not on the road. There were no skid marks before or after the scene, so the driver made no attempt to avoid him or slow down after the impact. There were broken pieces of glass and plastic. Several tiny light blue paint chips, and a broken side view mirror. Because of the condition of these pieces it was clear they were deposited at the time of the impact. Meaning, they weren't there from a past crash."

"Is that all?" Elsa-May asked.

Kelly turned to them and interlaced the fingers of both of his hands before he placed them on the desk in front of him. "It's a fact that most hit-and-run accidents go unsolved. From his injuries, we know he was facing the direction opposite to the car when he was hit. He wouldn't have seen it coming. Toxicology tests for drugs and alcohol came back negative."

"But he was at a bar," Ettie said. "Surely he would've been drinking."

He looked back at the screen. "No. From what I just read in the report, the barman said he didn't have one drink. What's more, he said Wayne never drank. He used to come in for the ladies."

"So, why wasn't he driving his own car if he wasn't drinking?" Ettie asked.

"I'm not certain he had a car," Kelly said.

"Why was he walking late at night after he'd been driven home?" Elsa-May asked.

He pinched his eyebrows together and looked back at the screen. "It's possible he could've met someone who asked him to meet him somewhere. He died only one quarter of a mile from his home."

"Someone must've called him and said meet them out on that road and then they were going to go somewhere together," Ettie said. "That's what we surmised last time."

"Yes, something like that." Kelly nodded.

"Did you check his phone history from the phone company?"

"Just give me a moment." He looked back at the computer.

"I'm sorry, this wasn't my case when they were re-investigating it and the original case was before my time. Looks like nothing came from his phone history. Back then mobile phones weren't in use. Not like they are now. He only had a landline, so those kinds of searches aren't as useful as they are these days. You see back then, many people had access to any one phone. With mobile phones, generally only one person uses them." The phone on his desk rang, and he picked up the receiver. "I'll be right there." He hung up. "Excuse me a moment. I'll be two minutes." He walked out of the office buttoning up his jacket.

Ettie gave Elsa-May her notebook and then quickly moved around to sit in Kelly's seat.

"Ettie, what are you doing?" Elsa-May hissed.

"Looking up dates. Write this down." Kelly still had the screen open and she read out the date of the accident, and the date of Abner admitting to the crime years later. She scrolled down further, she knew how to do that from using the computer in the library.

"Hurry up, would you?" Elsa-May urged.

"I'm just getting this to fill in the blanks in my book. I don't have the dates written down." Ettie moved away and when she was nearly back in her seat, Kelly walked through the door and glared at her.

"I just dropped my pen," she said before she sat back down next to Elsa-May.

"I've got to interview someone now, so I'll have to ask you to leave. I will be in touch soon."

"Thank you."

"Yes, we appreciate your help," Ettie said.

They headed out of the station and as Elsa-May walked down the steps, she said, "What were you doing back there, Ettie? Don't ever make me so scared again. What would've happened if he'd seen you doing that? He'd never help us again."

"Sometimes in life, Elsa-May, you've got to take a risk."

Elsa-May shook her head with her lips clamped together.

"I'm working on a few things," Ettie said.

CHAPTER 13

EARLIER THAT DAY

"THANK YOU, Gabriel. I really do appreciate you taking the time to drive us around today," Selena stepped down from the buggy when they arrived at her bed-and-breakfast.

"I enjoyed it. And I'll pick you up tomorrow morning, okay?"

"Oh, I forgot my car. It's still at your place."

"That's okay. It'll be safe there."

"Okay, thanks." She preferred to keep the car garaged, but it wouldn't have been garaged even if she'd had it with her. It would have spent the night in the parking lot along with the other guests' cars. It made sense to leave it at his house. Anyway, she was too tired to go back and get it now. "What time tomorrow?"

"Nine?"

"Perfect."

"What are you doing for dinner? I'll take you out somewhere."

She smiled at the offer. "That's okay. I think they do meals

79

here for dinner."

"You sure? I won't cook it myself." He laughed. "I'll take you somewhere nice."

"That's fine. I'll see you tomorrow."

"Okay. Bye, Selena."

She stepped away from the buggy and the horse clip-clopped away.

When she was back in the safety of her room, she pulled out her phone to call Eugene. She was taken aback when a woman answered the phone. "Hi, it's Selena …"

"Hi, Selena, it's Elga. Eugene's in a meeting right now."

"Oh, okay. Can you have him call me back?"

"Sure."

"Thanks, bye." She ended the call. Normally, he allowed his calls on his private cell phone to go to voicemail.

She shook her head and told herself not to be so suspicious about the lack of background noise. She still found it hard to believe her luck that a man like Eugene could be interested in somebody like her. She imagined he would have some socialite type of woman with a great figure and an outgoing personality. When her phone beeped she looked to see a few text messages from him. Looking at the times they'd been sent, she realized she'd only just gotten into the network reception range and he'd sent all those messages earlier.

The place she was staying only provided breakfast. She had told Gabriel they served dinner as an easy way to get out of his invitation.

Soon, she found the only place that delivered food was a pizzeria. Now she missed her car. She ended up getting a pizza delivered even though it was one of her least favorite foods.

When Selena woke up the next morning, she grabbed her phone. There were no missed calls from Eugene. She sent a text message. *Are you awake?* There was no reply, so she called him.

He answered with an angry, "What are you doing? Do you know the time?"

"Six o'clock. You always wake up at this time."

"I had a meeting last night that went on until after midnight."

"A dinner meeting?"

"Yes."

It seemed she was always doing the wrong thing. "Sorry, do you want me to call you back later?"

"I'll call *you*. When are you coming home?"

"I thought you wanted me to stay for a few days."

"I do. I am just asking for an approximate date you'll be home. I'm not looking to be told what I said. We both know what I said."

"I'll be there in a couple of days, maybe three, um, maybe four," she added when she remembered how slow everything was at getting done there.

"Okay. Is everything going all right?"

"Yes, pretty good."

He yawned. "Are you relaxing?"

"I am. I'm feeling very relaxed," she lied through her teeth. She was anything but relaxed. She was tense and worried, and now bloated thanks to eating a whole pizza by herself the night before.

"Have you got an approximate house value yet?"

She had forgotten all about getting a realtor to put a value on the house. Eugene still didn't know that there was a family living in the house and paying rent when they felt like it. "I'm getting onto that today."

"Great. Let me know when you get a price. I don't

imagine it's too much, but it will help toward buying a house together."

"So, we are buying something together?"

"Of course we are. I'll sell the apartment, you sell that and we'll buy something with the money."

"I thought you didn't want to put something in my name."

"It won't be in your name, it'll be in my name."

"If I'm putting money toward it why would it solely be in your name?"

"It'll be in a company name, or a family trust. I haven't figured it out yet."

She didn't like the sound of that. If they divorced, she was pretty certain her money would not be classed as a joint asset. She had to protect herself. "We need to talk about these kind of things before we marry, and before I decide what to do with the house."

"We do need to have a discussion, but not so early in the morning. Call me back at a reasonable time of day. There's another call." He hung up on her.

Was it her, or had his personality changed since she'd been away? He was behaving like a person that she didn't like, much less want to marry. She rubbed her head wondering why he wanted the money in his name, or a company name; it didn't make sense.

She knew Eugene worked hard and so she decided to just put it down to stress from the job. He was working on a few hard cases and that must've been taking a toll—that plus the lack of sleep must be giving him the bad moods. She pushed him out of her mind and made a mental note to call the realtor today in between visiting Wayne's sister and whatever else happened.

She changed into comfortable pants and blouse and headed to the dining room for breakfast.

CHAPTER 14

AFTER A LIGHT BREAKFAST, Selena waited by the window in her room. From there she could see vehicles coming and going. After waiting ten minutes, she grabbed her phone, threw it into her bag and headed outside. When she looked up the road, she was pleased to see the buggy in the distance. As it drew closer, she saw Gabriel's smiling face. Even though he was slightly annoying and rather odd, he was a happy person to be around.

"Sorry, I'm a little late," he said when he stopped the buggy near her.

"It's fine. You're not that late."

"That's true. How are you this lovely day?"

She looked at his smiling face and felt much better. "I'm good. And you?"

"Good. And, you're looking lovely today."

"Really?"

"Yes." He walked his buggy up the road. "You're a very nice lady."

"Oh, thank you. I think."

Glancing over at her, he said, "It's true. You are."

"I'm happy you think so."

"I'd be mad if I didn't. You're an amazing-looking woman and I'm happy to spend another day with you. It's even better that you're Abner's daughter."

"Granddaughter," she corrected.

He threw his head back and laughed. "I'm always getting that wrong, aren't I?"

"Yes, you are."

"You're way too young to be his daughter."

"That's true." Frustration set in at the pace the buggy was going. It would be faster if she got out and walked. "Can this horse go a little faster?"

"You're in a hurry?"

"It's just that I'm used to going by car, and this is so slow."

"I'll go faster."

"Yes please."

The horse broke into a trot when he called out a word that sounded like it was German. He then looked at Selena and smiled. He was making no attempt to hide he was smitten by her. Since Gabriel was so handsome, it was a well-needed confidence boost for Selena.

THEY COLLECTED Ettie and Elsa-May and headed off to Jill James's place as planned. "Now, from memory. Jill lived here with two of her brothers, and then one moved out and the other died. Last time we talked to her, she'd been married and divorced and was still living in the same place. I do hope she hasn't moved," Ettie said.

"Was that five years ago?"

"Yes, we met her around the time your grandfather confessed."

From the backseat of the buggy, Selena held her head. It was a lot to take in and she was on her own with this. Her mother didn't seem to think it was a big problem, and she certainly couldn't tell Eugene what she was going through.

"This is it," Gabriel said.

It seemed like it had taken forever to get there.

When they got to the door. Elsa-May elbowed Ettie out of the way so she could knock. She then stood square in the doorway so she'd be first one the woman would see.

A small lady in her fifties or early sixties opened the door after several knocks. She stared at them, and before she could say anything, Elsa-May said, "Do you remember us?"

"Yes, I do. You were asking questions about my brother."

"That's right, and this is my sister, Ettie, who was with me at the time. This is a friend, Gabriel, and another friend of ours Selena. We're here because Selena is the granddaughter of the man who claimed to have run over your brother."

"Oh." The woman craned her neck to get a better look at Selena.

Ettie said, "We need to ask you a couple more questions if that's okay."

"I guess so. Come inside." She took them into the living room. Once they were seated, Jill said, "What is it you want to ask me? I don't know that I know anything. I never thought that man ran my brother down."

"Firstly, I want to thank you for talking with us. I don't know if my grandfather accidentally ran over your brother or not. Everyone seems to think he didn't. I didn't really know him. I only met him once in my life, but if he didn't do it, I feel strongly about proving it."

"You're not responsible for what your grandfather did or didn't do," Jill said.

"Thank you. Do you know anybody who would have had reason to harm your brother?"

"As I told your friends last time. I don't. It wasn't me. There was talk that he and I were having an argument about a dog and yes, we were having an argument about the dog. It was his dog, and he left me with a six-thousand-dollar vet bill when a car hit the dog. I told him if he didn't pay, I was keeping the dog and I did,"

"Do you still have the dog?" Elsa-May asked.

"Unfortunately, the dog passed away. I did find out recently, and this is something I didn't know last time, Wayne was blackmailing someone. There was some secret or other and then there were his constant stream of girlfriends. Any one of them could've done it."

"Who was he blackmailing?" Ettie asked.

"That is something I don't know."

Selena asked, "Have you told the police?"

"No. I didn't think of it in connection with the accident. Do you think I should tell them?"

"How did you know he was blackmailing someone?" Elsa-May asked.

"I guess I didn't, and I don't know for sure and I certainly don't have any proof. It was just a rumor that I heard when I ran into some friends of his. I heard it was a man he was blackmailing, and that's all I know."

Later, just as they were leaving, Jill said, "If Wayne's death wasn't an accident he might have been murdered by an angry woman. It wouldn't have been anything to do with the robbery."

Ettie's eyes opened wide. "Robbery?"

Elsa-May cut across Ettie, "How many of these angry women were there?"

"Hard to say."

Selena said, "Were any of these angry women Amish?"

"I believe at least one of them was." She chuckled. "I don't know that she was angry, but I know he was seeing an Amish woman somewhere along the way. I saw them together once."

WHEN THEY LEFT Jill's house and were discussing where to go next, Selena interrupted, "Is everyone keeping something from me?"

Gabriel turned around. "What do you mean?"

"My mother was in a relationship with this Wayne man, wasn't she?" She put her head in her hands. "This is terrible. This is such bad news. Then my grandfather must have thought she killed him and that's why he confessed. Why didn't I see that before? I'm so stupid. What if my mother killed a man?" She broke into sobs.

"I don't know that it's true," Gabriel said.

No one else was saying anything, so she knew at least part of it was true. She looked over at Ettie, who was sharing the backseat with her. "My mother was having a relationship with this man, wasn't she? Just tell me the truth please."

Ettie nodded. "It is true. She was having a relationship with Wayne."

Elsa-May added, "That's what we found out. We went back to Terrence's house yesterday, fearing he wasn't telling us the entire truth because you were there. It was a secret and illicit relationship. She was still in the community at that point."

"This is dreadful. Gabriel, will you wait while I call my mother?"

"Sure. We're doing this for you, Selena. None of us has anywhere else to be."

Selena grabbed her bag and jumped out of the buggy. Once she was out of earshot, she called her mother.

"Selena?"

"Yes, it's me."

"I've told you never to call when my shows are on. Luckily you called in an ad break. What is it?"

"For once, forget your stupid shows. This is way more important. Mother, I need the truth. Were you having a relationship with Wayne Robinson?"

"Now there's a name I haven't heard for a while."

"Did you know him?"

"Yes. We had a brief dalliance, and then I moved away and married your father. Why are you asking about this now?"

"He was murdered, Mom. Run down in cold blood in the street."

"I know that."

Selena looked over her shoulder, not wanting the people in the buggy to hear her shouting, but it might've been too late for that. "The police asked questions of your father a few years ago and he must've thought *you* killed Wayne and that's why he said *he* did it. Don't you get it? He was protecting you."

"Now wait a minute, you're jumping to conclusions. Why would I have killed Wayne?"

"It makes sense. Anyone might've thought the same in his position."

"Are you blaming me?" her mother asked.

"Did you have reason to want him dead?"

"You can't be asking your mother things like this."

"I'm trying to get to the bottom of things."

"I don't like the way you're going about it. These Amish people are turning you against me. I have to go. Call me tomorrow when you're in a better mood." Her mother ended the call.

Now things were getting worse. What if her mother was the one who was responsible for Wayne's death? Things were bad enough thinking her grandfather did it. How bad would it be if the guilty party was her own mother and she'd sat back and let Abner take the blame?

"She admitted she was in a relationship with him," Selena

said as she climbed back into the buggy. "My grandfather obviously thought she killed him. No one wants to go to jail for nothing. He must've thought he was protecting her."

"That's what we thought too, but on all our visits he never admitted to it."

Selena looked at Gabriel as he held the reins. "Gabriel, did he say anything to you about it?"

"No, and I asked him a few times myself why he said he did it. He was stubborn and he refused to talk about it. Normally, he wouldn't stop talking."

"That's why my mother left the community when she did. I wonder if she left right after the accident." Selena sobbed and Ettie patted her shoulder.

"Do you want to continue this, or have a rest?" Ettie asked gently.

"I don't know."

"Where to now, Selena? Do you want to continue or leave things be?" Gabriel looked concerned.

"I don't know. I just don't know."

Elsa-May twisted around to look at Selena from the front seat. "How about we leave that much as done for the day, and we'll take it up tomorrow, if you still want to. We'll leave it up to you."

Selena nodded. "I think I need some time by myself to figure some things out."

THEY DROVE in silence to Ettie and Elsa-May's house, and then Gabriel drove back toward his house. "Shall I take you back to your bed-and-breakfast?"

"No. Just take me to my car, thanks."

He stared at her. "Are you sure you're alright to drive?"

"Yes, I'll be fine."

"Can I do anything for you or get you anything?"

"No thanks, Gabriel. I really feel the need to be alone."

"I'm worried about you. Can I stop by in the morning to check on you?"

"Sure. Yes, that would be fine."

"I'll stop by around nine and then we'll take things from there."

Selena bit on the inside of her mouth to stop herself from crying. "Thank you. That sounds good. Instead of that, though, I'll come to you."

"Okay. I'll be waiting."

CHAPTER 15

"HELLO, IS THIS MS. LEHMAN?"

Selena was still trying to wake up after a restless night's sleep. She sat bolt upright in bed at the official-sounding voice. She'd reached out and answered her phone thinking it was Eugene. "Yes, this is she."

"Detective Kelly here."

"Oh yes. Did you find out anything?"

"I found out something interesting, and I also had a visit from Mrs. Lutz and Mrs. Smith yesterday. Is it possible for you to meet me at their house at eleven today?"

"Yes, I can do that. Can you tell me anything now?"

"It is best that I tell everybody at one time."

"Yes of course. Thanks for looking into it for me. It means a lot to me." She knew he was probably doing it more for the old ladies who were his friends rather than she, but nevertheless, she was grateful.

She suddenly remembered she had ended the conversation with Gabriel from the day before by saying she'd come to him. She swiftly gathered her things and drove to his place.

When she walked up the steps to the front door of Gabriel's house, a dreadful burning smell filled the air. The front door suddenly opened and smoke billowed out around Gabriel. "What's this?" She waved the smoke away with her hand.

"I was delayed, but I was coming to see you soon. I was concerned—I thought you'd be here before now. How are you?"

"I'm fine. Sorry I'm later than planned—I'd forgotten that the plan was me coming here. What's all this smoke?"

"This, well, it was my breakfast," he said with a wry grin.

Selena laughed. "Oh no. What was it?"

He laughed. "It was to be bacon on toast but I've managed to create burnt offerings."

She laughed along with him. "The detective friend of Ettie and Elsa-May's wants me to meet him at their house. Would you like to join us?"

"Yes, thank you. I would like that. What time did you say?" He flicked his dark hair over to one side.

"Eleven."

"Do I have time to try again with breakfast?"

"Um, sure. Would you like me to cook it for you?"

"You would?"

"Sure. Unless you want to risk burning your house down."

He laughed. "Come inside. I'll see what I can do about getting rid of this smoke, and I'll get you a clean frying pan."

"That would be a good start."

Selena fixed him eggs, toast and bacon and then sat down with him while he ate it.

When he'd taken his first mouthful, he nodded. "You're a good cook. I knew you would be."

She smiled and resisted asking him whether that was on the list of what he was looking for in a woman. All Amish women were good cooks. They'd been raised learning to cook and keep house.

"Are you sure you don't want anything?"

She shook her head. "I've had plenty already."

"Are you okay?"

Selena looked up at him surprised. "Yes, why?"

"You seem very quiet."

"I couldn't sleep. I had too many things on my mind. It was such a shock about my mother. Anyway, all I can do is find out all I can."

He nodded as he ate more of his breakfast.

"You don't work?"

When he finished his mouthful, he answered, "I do, but not every day. I have a store in town and my staff told me it runs better when I'm not there." He laughed. "There's a lot of other work involved with the store that doesn't actually involve being in the store. I do the ordering and keep the books. I can do that at night and from home."

She nodded. "That sounds like good work."

"I enjoy it the store too, when I'm there."

"What sort of shop is it?"

"It's mainly geared toward tourists. We sell quilts and other Amish handicrafts. "

"That sounds nice."

"Does it?"

"Yes." She was just trying to be polite. She didn't really care either way what he did; she was curious about how he was always available. "Can we please go in my car today?"

"Okay." He nodded.

"It's perfectly safe. I'm a good driver."

He stood and took his plate over to the sink and ran water over it. "How are we doing for time?"

"A lot better now that we can drive rather than take the buggy."

"Good. I'll just wash these dishes."

She rose to her feet. "I'll dry."

"No, sit down. It won't take a moment."

"I don't mind at all." She saw a tea towel on one side of the counter and took hold of it.

"I think that frying pan needs to be soaked for a few days." He picked it up and looked in it.

"I'd say so. Soak it with loads of detergent, and then you might need to scrape the black off it." Selena wondered why he'd never married, but wasn't in the mood to hear any sad stories. She was certain he'd have a few. He probably scared women off with his enthusiasm.

Once they'd done the small amount of washing up, they headed out to her car.

"I'm not worried about going in the car."

She smiled at him as she clipped her seatbelt. "Put your seatbelt on."

He did what he was told. "I'm sure you're a good driver. I'm sure you're good at everything you do, like cooking."

"I try to be." She started the engine.

"I hope your fiancé appreciates you."

"He does."

"He'd be a foolish man if he didn't."

As she fixed her eyes on the road ahead, she wondered if Eugene did appreciate her as much as he could. "You have to direct me."

"Soon, you'll need to take a right turn."

CHAPTER 16

ETTIE AND ELSA-MAY had just settled down with their knitting for the day.

"I do hope we see Selena again today."

"We might not. She was dreadfully upset over her mother's actions."

Ettie nodded. "That's in the past."

"Not to her. She only just found out about it."

Ettie jumped when there was a knock on their front door. She'd gone back to sitting on the more comfortable couch rather than the chair where she could see out the window.

"Who could that be?" Elsa-May asked looking at Ettie.

Ettie smiled. That was her sister's way of asking her if she would answer the door. "It could be a lot of people." Ettie left her knitting on the couch, pushed herself to her feet and walked to the door. She hoped it would be Selena and Gabriel, although she hadn't heard the clip-clopping of horse's hooves on the road. "Oh, Detective Kelly. Come right in."

"Hello, Mrs. Smith. Since your visit, I checked into some

things and came up with some interesting scenarios. I hope you don't mind, but I have Selena Lehman coming here at eleven. I just wasn't sure what she knows and doesn't know."

"It didn't seem right to keep things from her. She figured out her mother was having a relationship with Wayne." Snowy ran at Kelly, and Ettie scooped him up just in time. "Take a seat. I'll put Snowy outside."

Kelly had only just sat down when Ettie looked out the window to see a black car stopping outside her house with Gabriel in the passenger seat.

Soon, everyone was seated, and Kelly began, "Selena, I may be barking up the wrong tree here and I hope I don't offend you or your mother, but ..."

"What is it?"

"Mrs. Smith tells me you're aware of the relationship your mother was having with Wayne Robinson. Now if you look at the timeline of events, you were born six months after your mother relocated to New York and from the evidence I found, it doesn't seem like they met beforehand, but I suppose it's possible. If I had to take a guess, I'd say she married Mr. Lehman because she knew she was pregnant."

It was as Ettie feared. She'd sneaked a look at Selena's driver's license that time when the young woman had taken her phone to call her mother, leaving everyone else—and her bag—in the buggy. Her date of birth fit into things just as Kelly had said.

"No. I know what you're thinking and you've got it all wrong. My father was Frederick Lehman."

Kelly raised his hands. "Okay, I'm very sorry. Forgive me for what I said."

"That's what I was told. I know my mother married him after I was born. I was a few weeks old, but that doesn't mean he wasn't my real father."

Kelly nodded.

Selena's hand flew to her mouth. "Do you have any evidence other than the dates?"

"Frederick Lehman worked for a government firm and was there every day. He took his vacation days the day before your mother arrived in New York, so it seems he met her while he was on vacation and they must've quickly hit it off." He shook his head. "From the evidence of the timeline, it seems unlikely he was your biological father."

"I can't believe it."

"I'm not saying it's true. It might be true and it might not be, but I'm pretty certain that might be why she left the community when she did. Maybe Wayne didn't come to the party, so to speak, regarding his paternal responsibility and, in a rage, she ran him down."

"No!" Selena snapped. "There's no proof of that."

Kelly shook his head. "No, but you asked me to look into things and this is what I found."

Selena put her hand to her forehead, feeling an instant migraine coming.

"We didn't hear rumors of any kind at the time, did we, Elsa-May?"

Elsa-May shook her head vigorously. "I didn't hear a word about it. Although, I don't think that would be something she'd have gone around telling people and if she was about to leave the community, she certainly wouldn't have confided in anyone in the community."

"I just thought it was something you should know. I'll leave that information with you."

Selena leaped to her feet. "Why would you drop a bombshell like this on me?" Tears streamed down her face and she ran outside, crying.

Kelly's mouth dropped open. "I didn't mean to upset her."

Elsa-May shook her head so much her bottom lip wobbled. Then she set her gaze on Kelly. "How did you think she would take news like that?"

"I do think you should only tell her something like that if you know it's a certainty," said Ettie.

"It would be hard news for anyone to hear," Elsa-May said.

"The worst of it is …" Gabriel jumped to his feet. "You can't tell her one way or the other whether she's Wayne's daughter. You've thrown her whole life into doubt. I'll go after her."

"I'm sorry," Kelly said. "Tact has never been my strong point. I saw the dates and …"

"The damage is done now." Elsa-May shook her head once more.

"I just wanted to lay everything out on the table. If her mother was carrying Wayne's child, that establishes a motive for her mother."

Ettie nodded. "True, but all Selena was doing was trying to clear her grandfather's name. It's just a lot for her to take in. She knew her mother was in a relationship with him, but didn't think about the possibility of being a product of that relationship."

Elsa-May said, "We thought all along Abner was protecting someone. It makes sense that what you just said is true, Detective Kelly."

He finally looked up and rubbed his forehead. "I agree. And Ms. Lehman could request DNA testing from Wayne's brother if she wants to know the truth."

Ettie could see that Kelly was genuinely upset from the reaction he'd gotten from Selena.

SELENA HAD WALKED DOWN AS FAR as the corner of the road.

"Wait up, Selena."

She wiped her eyes and then stopped and waited for Gabriel.

"I'm sorry you had to hear that news like that," he said.

"It can't be true."

"It might not be."

"My father was Frederick." Her whole world was ordered by who her parents were. If what the detective said was true and her father was Wayne, she wouldn't know who she was. All she knew about Wayne was that he did odd jobs for people, possibly stole alpacas, and was a ladies' man. That would mean he didn't care about her mother, or her. She searched her mind for any clue to Frederick not being her real father and couldn't come up with a thing. Then there was the evidence Kelly had just presented, and it had to be considered, but her mother and Frederick could've met each other before she moved to New York.

She sobbed, and he put his arm around her shoulders. "It'll be okay. It's all a shock. Why don't you call your mother and ask her?"

"I couldn't. I couldn't ask her something like that." She was grateful that Gabriel had come out of the house to see if she was okay. Blinking back tears, she looked back at the house. "We should go back."

"Are you okay?"

"No."

"Take a couple of deep breaths. You came to learn the truth, right?"

"No, I only came here to look at the house and have some time to myself. I didn't come for this nightmare."

∾

"ANOTHER THING we should tell you is that we found out that Wayne was blackmailing someone," Ettie told Kelly.

Elsa-May added, "It might not be true, but that's what we heard."

"Who was he blackmailing?"

"All we know is that it was a man. And some man was angry with him, and they could've been one and the same. Or maybe not."

"Hmm. That doesn't really give me much to go on."

When Selena and Gabriel walked back into the house, Kelly bounded to his feet. "I'm so sorry to blurt out what I did."

"It's okay. I said I wanted to find out the truth, and I'm probably getting closer to it." Selena sat back down next to Ettie, and Gabriel sat on the chair closest to Selena.

"Is there anything else you need to tell me, Detective Kelly?" Selena asked.

"What did Frederick Lehman and Wayne Robinson have in common?" Kelly asked.

"My mother, I guess."

"In that case, is it possible that Wayne was blackmailing your father about something? Something to do with your mother?"

"Wayne was blackmailing someone?" Selena asked.

"Yes, we believe he was," Elsa-May said. "Remember when we spoke with Jill, she told us she'd heard talk about it."

"I wasn't aware they knew each other. I suppose we could guess a thousand different scenarios, but how would we know which one was the right one?" Selena shook her head. "I'm going to call my mother and ask her for the truth."

Kelly slowly nodded. She took her cell phone and walked out of the house and leaned against their fence. Her mother answered quickly. "Mom, I've been looking into things as you know and I have a question and I need the complete truth."

"I always tell you the truth."

Selena took a deep breath. "Who is my real father? My birth father?" When there was silence from the other end of the line, she knew. "Mother?"

"You know who he was."

"He was Wayne Robinson?"

Again, there was silence until a croaky voice said, "It's true."

Selena was lost for words, and couldn't speak. Her whole life had been a lie, a sham. She made the mental effort to hold herself together. "Was Wayne blackmailing Frederick?"

"What for?"

"Answer please, Mother."

"This whole thing is making me upset. I'll have to go."

Selena's birth certificate had named Frederick as her father. Feeling sick to her stomach she walked back inside. "My mother confirmed what you said. It *is* true," she said to Kelly before she sat down. "My father ... the man I thought was my father has passed away, and Wayne Robinson is dead too."

Elsa-May shook her head. "That makes things extremely difficult to find out the truth."

Ettie glared at Elsa-May for being so insensitive.

"It does," Elsa-May said to Ettie. "It makes it hard to find out the truth when everyone's dead."

"Not everyone," Kelly said. "I'll be following up a few leads."

"Care to share them with us?" Selena asked.

"Not at this time."

Selena frowned at him. "Yes, but you can't be treating this as a high priority."

"That's true. I have murders I'm following up, but still I'm doing what I can in the meantime. Again, I'm sorry to drop a bombshell on you, Selena."

She nodded. "I'd rather know the truth even if it hurts. Better that than to believe a lie, like the lies I've been living my whole life."

"Are you okay to drive, Selena?" Gabriel asked.

"Yes, I'll drive you home now."

CHAPTER 17

LATER THAT SAME DAY, Ettie and Elsa-May were talking about Selena and the hit-and-run that killed Wayne Robinson.

"That answers the question about who one of those Amish women were."

"We already knew that."

"In Selena's mind, I'm talking about."

"You're right but the other thing is someone mentioned two Amish women, so my question is ..."

"Who was the other Amish woman?"

"Correct. This is new information and I think we should try to find out as much as we can for the poor young girl. She's obviously very upset."

"That's right. How will we find out? Have you got any bright ideas?" Elsa-May asked.

"I do. We could visit Kelly and find out if he's got anything in his file about an Amish woman."

Elsa-may frowned. "Couldn't you have asked him that while he was here?"

"I didn't think of it."

"I'm sure we've asked him already. *Jah,* I'm sure we have. He was here for a long time considering how busy he is. He's not going to be happy about seeing us twice in two days especially if we're asking him the same thing twice."

"Aren't we saving taxpayers' money by helping him find out who committed this crime?"

"I doubt Kelly will see it that way. He'll think we're getting in his way and therefore wasting taxpayer's money because we're slowing him down."

Ettie chuckled. "You forgot something. He's not actually officially working on this case. They stopped working on it when Abner confessed and went to prison."

"That makes it worse, though."

Ettie scratched her ear. "Very true."

"When do you want to see him? Shall we wait until tomorrow?"

"How about now?"

"Okay." Elsa-May stared at her knitting by her feet. "This isn't getting any of my knitting done."

Ettie was pleased about that. "No one said it was, but we're helping by what we're doing."

Elsa-May sighed. "Tell it to the hospital. I told them they were getting these teddies weeks ago."

"What we need are some more knitting ladies to help us."

"We could do with more. We can ask around at the next meeting."

"And why don't we also ask around if anybody knows anything about Abner and his confession? Perhaps the bishop can make an announcement about us that if anybody knows anything about it to come and talk to us?"

"Brilliant, Ettie."

"Really? You think that's brilliant?"

"I do. That will save us going around to everybody and

asking questions and surely someone would come forward if they know anything."

Ettie nodded. "I hope so."

"Are we ready to go?"

"We need to eat first."

Elsa-May said, "You call a taxi and I'll meet you down the end of the road with a snack."

"Okay. Make it a big one." Ettie headed down the end of the road to call a taxi. She waited and then a few minutes later, she saw Elsa-May carrying a paper sack.

"They're peanut butter and jelly sandwiches."

"Sounds delightful."

Elsa-May's mouth turned down at the corners. "You're joking, aren't you?"

"Anything sounds good right now, I'm so hungry. We didn't have enough cake for the visitors and us to eat, but I noticed it didn't stop you."

"Nonsense, there was plenty, and anyway, that's why I cut small portions. We finished off the rest of the roast beef last night, or we could've had that on our sandwiches, with relish."

"Peanut butter and jelly is fine."

As they stood there munching on the sandwiches, a taxi came into view.

"That'll be for us," Elsa-May said.

"Just one question, Elsa-May."

She peered at her younger sister. "What's that?"

"Where are we going?"

Elsa-May frowned. "Don't you know?"

Ettie shook her head. They'd talked about the case from so many angles she'd forgotten what they had decided.

"Me either. Why don't we visit Ava?"

Ettie smiled. "Okay. Let's do that. After the *boppli's* born, she'll be too busy for us to visit at least for the first few weeks."

"She can give us a new perspective on everything that's been going on."

CHAPTER 18

SELENA WAS BACK at the bed-and-breakfast and the rain was pouring down. She was still trying to get her head around how everyone in her life had lied to her. When her cell phone beeped, she was pleased to see from the caller ID that it was Eugene.

She took a deep breath and told herself to sound cheerful, so he'd have no idea something was wrong. "Hi."

"Now tell me please, have you called the realtor yet?"

She was going to explode. The realtor was the last thing on her mind. "There's been so many things going on here, and I've been talking to so many people..."

"About what?"

She couldn't tell him until she knew the truth for certain.

"Nothing. I'll tell you when I see you."

"Is there anything wrong?"

He'd guessed. "There's been a lot going on and I'll have a fair bit to tell you." All she wanted from him was reassurance and some niceness. "Why can't you ever treat me with respect? Lately you've been reprimanding me like a child. I am an adult."

107

He chuckled. "That's why you're good for me. You challenge me."

"Yes, but sometimes I need a soft place to fall. I need some love and some understanding."

"I give you that, but don't get it back. You're very needy, and sometimes I have nothing left to give. Sometimes I think this relationship is all about your wants and your needs. What about mine? I need you to be more efficient in the way you go about things. If you were a switched-on efficient kind of a gal we would be having a different conversation, and you would be back here by now."

"Gal? Since when have you used that word?"

"You're always deflecting what I say. I told you what I'm unhappy about and you have nothing to say. I resent the fact that you're not working and I'm having to spend an absolute fortune on the ridiculously expensive wedding planner. So, what do you think about that? There, I finally said it. I've been holding back."

"I have to go. I've got another call coming." She hung up on him and threw her phone at the wall. It bounced from the wall and landed on the carpet. If he'd been a decent fiancé, she could've shared what was going on in her life.

A few minutes later, he called her back.

"I'm sorry, Selena. I didn't mean those things."

"So, now what—you're holding back again? What am I supposed to believe? All I ask is that you respect me and treat me as an equal."

"Okay, we'll not fight when we can't kiss and make up. I didn't call you to have a fight. Just relax and try to have some fun."

"I've only met Amish people."

He chuckled. "Well, that means you'll be staying out of trouble. Have a rest in your hotel room and read one of those books you like."

"I'm at a bed-and-breakfast. I emailed you the address when I made the booking."

She was pleased that he was talking softer and kinder to her now. "I might read a book. I brought a couple with me."

"We're both stressed and we just need to take a breather."

She was still hurt by all the things he had said, but she didn't want to talk about it now. "I have things to tell you."

"I'll look forward to hearing them. I do love you, you know."

"Yes, I know. And I love you too."

"I really do have an incoming call." Again, he hung up without saying goodbye. That was something she was used to by now.

~

ETTIE AND ELSA-MAY waved at Ava's mother as she left Ava's house in her buggy when they approached in the taxi.

When they reached the house, Ettie said, "That's good timing. It looks like we're getting to see Ava by ourselves without sharing her with visitors. There are no buggies here."

They left the taxi and Ettie pushed the door open and stuck her head in. "Hello."

"Come in," Ava called out from somewhere within the house. "Don't make me stand up."

Elsa-May giggled. *"Nee,* you stay there."

They walked in and found her on one of the couches looking uncomfortable.

"How have you been?" Ettie said as they sat on either side of her.

"Fat and useless. This *boppli's* already five days past the due date and I'm impatient and sick of waiting. I can't do this any longer, but I have to. I feel bloated, cranky, and talk about kicking!" She shook her head. "It hurts. He drags his heel down the side of my ribs. I'm sure it's a boy."

Ettie and Elsa-May laughed.

"How about trying some knitting to pass the time?" Elsa-May asked.

"Oh, she doesn't want to knit boring old squares, Elsa-May."

Elsa-May's lip curled at her sister's words. "Knitting is not boring, Ettie. It gives one a sense of purpose. It's a way to measure the days, and it's an achievement. I've got so much to show for my days. What do you have?"

Ettie's lips turned down at the corners.

Ava interrupted the exchange, "The kettle's just boiled. Would you like hot tea?"

"Not for us, we just had one. We can get one for you," Ettie said.

"Nee denke. I just had one too. Tell me what's going on with you two?"

"Well, we've lots going on, if you're up for a long story."

"I'd love it. I need to take my mind off everything." She placed both hands on her belly.

Ettie and Elsa-May filled her in on what was happening with Selena and the crime her grandfather had admitted to. Ava gasped when she learned who the real father was. Then she was told to keep that information to herself.

"Oh, that's dreadful for the poor girl, thinking someone else was her father for so long."

"Jah, she put on a brave face but inside I'm sure she's got mixed feelings about it." Ettie shook her head.

"More than that, Ettie. She said that her whole life was a lie."

Ava nodded. "Kate would've done it for the best reasons. For one thing, Selena's real father was dead by then and she would've wanted her daughter to think that the new husband was the father."

"Well, it might take Selena some time to see that point of view," Elsa-May said.

"I wish I knew something that would help you find out who did it," Ava said.

"Ettie had the idea of asking the bishop to make an announcement at the meeting for anyone who might know anything to talk with us."

"*Jah.* That's a good idea."

"I hope someone knows something. The detective thinks that it wasn't accidental because Wayne was walking out on a lonely stretch of road rather than driving his car. Kelly has the idea that someone called him, or met with him, and asked him to meet them there. There were no witnesses or anything."

"What about his phone records or something?"

Ettie breathed out heavily. "Nothing was found."

"Maybe someone at the bar did come into contact with him and had arranged to meet him on that lonely road."

"I do hope we get to the bottom of things. Selena is so upset and then that makes me sad to continue this investigation."

"Where's Jeremiah?" Elsa-May asked.

"I sent him to the stores to get some things, so we don't have to shop for the first few weeks after the birth. Just a few last-minute things. Oh, have you tried going to the bar and asking around? Did you ask at the bar he was driven home from?"

Elsa-May shook her head. "It was too long ago. Around twenty-five years ago. I doubt the same people would be there."

"It's worth a try," Ettie said.

Elsa-May frowned as she stared at Ettie. "You want me to go into a bar?"

"We'll go together. It's worth a try. What do we have to lose?"

"Only our reputation if someone sees us."

Ettie giggled. "Where's your sense of adventure?"

Elsa-May frowned. "I never had one."

"Oh, I wish I could go with you. You will tell me what happens with all this, won't you?"

"Jah, of course we will." Ettie patted her hand. "Now, Elsa-May, are we going to that bar, or not?"

Elsa-May sighed. "We'd have to find the name of it. I'm not going from bar to bar looking for the right one."

"I've got it written down in my notebook, along with the name of the bartender."

"How did you get that?" Elsa-May drew her eyebrows together.

"From Kelly's computer. I remembered it and wrote it down. I've got the name of the bar and the man's name. I hope he still works there. All we have to do is find the address of the bar from the phone book."

"All right. I'll have to go with you to keep you out of trouble."

Ettie smiled. *"Denke,* Elsa-May."

LATER THAT AFTERNOON, Ava's husband drove Ettie and Elsa-May home. Just as he drove away and Ettie and Elsa-May were nearly inside, Stacey from next door ran over to them.

They stopped and waited. Ettie was the first to speak. "Hello. We haven't seen you around, Stacey. Is everything okay?"

"Everything's okay now, but Greville has had to stay in the hospital."

"What's wrong with him?" Ettie stepped closer to her.

"He had pains in the stomach and they found out it was food poisoning."

"That's dreadful. How long has he been in the hospital?" Elsa-May asked.

"Five days, and I don't mind telling you I've had a nice rest from him. He can be very overbearing at times."

"In what way?"

"I shouldn't say. I suppose he's good most of the time. He does fly into rages of temper, though, and he is very aggressive."

"Sorry to hear that," Elsa-May said.

Ettie stepped away from her. "I hope Greville gets better."

"He is better, but they just want to keep him in for observation. You can visit him if you'd like."

Ettie and Elsa-May looked at one another.

"Um, we would under other circumstances, but we're quite busy."

"With what?" Stacey peered into Ettie's face.

"We have a visitor in town and she's taking up a lot of our time."

Elsa-May turned toward the house and pulled on Ettie's sleeve. "Excuse us, Stacey. We do hope your husband fully recovers."

"Yes, he will."

They both smiled at her and hurried into the house. Once they were inside, they made sure they shut the door behind them.

"What do you think that was about, Ettie?" Elsa-May whispered.

Ettie hurried to the window and peered out. "I don't know, but she's walking back to her place now. Maybe she's lonely. Remember she said Greville wouldn't allow her friends to the house?"

113

"We can't be her friends. She's an *Englischer* for one. And two, I just feel she can't be trusted. There's something odd about her."

Ettie nodded and then sat down on her chair by the window watching Stacey until she went into her house and closed the front door.

CHAPTER 19

ETTIE AND ELSA-MAY waited until dark and then headed to the bar.

When they walked in, everyone turned around and stared at them. Ettie pushed Elsa-May forward to ask for Chuck Danecomb.

"Excuse me, would a Chuck Danecomb still work here?" Elsa-May asked the young bartender.

"Yeah, he owns the place. He's out back."

"Can we talk to him? It won't take a moment." Ettie sat down on a barstool until she got a filthy look from her sister.

"I'll fetch him." The bar tender hurried off.

"Don't look too comfortable, Ettie. We don't belong in a place like this."

Ettie got off the barstool, and they both stood at the bar waiting. A minute later, a large bald man, with colorful tattoos on his neck and both arms, walked toward them.

"You want to see me?"

Ettie said, "Yes, we're wondering if we might have a quick word with you about a man who used to come in here, Wayne Robinson."

SAMANTHA PRICE

He slowly nodded. "Sure. Let's sit over here. Would you ladies like a drink of soda, or something?"

"No thank you," Elsa-May said quickly.

Chuck walked them to a booth, slid in one side, and the two ladies sat opposite.

"Chuck's an unusual name," Elsa-May said.

"That's the name they christened me with." He smiled at them. "What would you like to know about Robinson?"

"He came here a lot?" Ettie asked.

"Yeah. He was here the night he died. That's going back in time. Those were the good days."

"Who was he talking to that night? Do you remember?"

"No, I can't say I do. Why do you wanna know?"

Elsa-May took over. "It's a long story. His daughter is asking about him."

"Daughter? I didn't know he had one."

Ettie licked her lips, and hoped a member of their community wouldn't see them. "Was there someone, anyone, who might have wished him harm?"

"Well, this is just a rumor. It was said Wayne knew someone who had pulled a bank job and got away with a lot of money. Others say it was Wayne himself. Whoever it was, they supposedly got away with millions."

"Millions?"

"Yes. They robbed safe-deposit boxes, so there was no telling exactly how much they got away with. Many around here say Wayne was in on it with someone else. There were lots of stories going around."

Ettie stared at the man. If Wayne knew about the robbery, he could've been killed to silence him. Or if he'd been one of the robbers, maybe someone had wanted a larger share of the money. Then she recalled that Wayne's sister had mentioned something about a robbery and mentally kicked herself for not inquiring further.

116

He looked at them both in turn. "I don't want to get involved with the cops. Okay?"

"We won't say anything." Elsa-May leaned forward.

"I know he was involved in some way. He had more money than usual, but I don't know that he had millions. Maybe he drove the getaway car or something."

"Do you know who he was involved with?" Ettie asked.

He leaned back slightly. "Why are you asking all this? Why didn't his daughter come?"

"It's a long story, but she's also trying to clear her grandfather's name. You see her grandfather confessed that he was the one who killed Wayne."

He shook his head. "Can't help you, sorry. I don't know who Wayne was in it with, but he was an opportunist. He'd pick up work wherever he could, whether it was an honest day's work or the other."

"Dishonest work?" Ettie asked.

"Yes."

"Thank you. You've been very helpful."

Elsa-May slid out of the booth, and the man said, "Stick around have a drink."

"We should go," Ettie said, "But thank you."

WHEN THE SISTERS were traveling home in the taxi, Ettie was very upset.

"Kelly would've known about the robbery, surely," Elsa-May whispered to Ettie in the backseat.

"You'd think so. *Jah*, he definitely would've."

"Why did he keep it from us?"

Ettie was silent while she thought for a moment. "I don't know, but why don't we keep it to ourselves for the moment and not let on to Kelly that we've found out?"

Elsa-May stared at her sister. "Why?"

"I don't know yet." Ettie sighed.

"Did you believe the man, or do you think he was just having fun with a couple of old ladies?" Elsa-May asked.

"Do you remember that Terrence also said something about a robbery, or it could've been Jill? Someone said something about a robbery."

"I don't remember."

"Well, I know one way to find out if he was or wasn't telling us the truth."

"How?"

"The public library. We'll go there tomorrow, look on the computer, and see if there was a robbery around that time like he described."

Elsa-May said, *"Jah*, we'll go there first thing tomorrow. After that we'll stop by and see if Ava's had the *boppli* yet."

"Good idea. We'll have to wait until Monday, though. And, we'll be seeing Ava at the meeting because tomorrow's Sunday."

Elsa-May chuckled. "I forgot what day it is."

CHAPTER 20

SELENA WAS STILL upset over her day and even more upset about Eugene. She'd refused a dinner invitation from Gabriel and now she regretted it. Gabriel was always happy and right now she needed her mood lifted.

Before she talked herself out of it, she got in her car and started driving toward Gabriel's house. Several minutes later, she stood at his front door. She was just summoning the courage to knock, when the door opened. He stood there smiling at her. "Is that dinner invitation still open?" she asked.

"It certainly is."

"Please don't tell me you were thinking of cooking it?"

He laughed. "No. I know a nice restaurant run by a friend of mine. I'll take you there."

"Okay, but only if I can drive you."

He frowned and looked over at the car. "All right. We'll go in your car."

He closed the front door.

"Are you ready?" she asked him, noticing he didn't even lock the door.

SAMANTHA PRICE

"Yes. Unless …" He looked down at his clothes. "You wanted me to wear something better?"

"No. You're fine as you are. It's just a casual restaurant, isn't it?"

"Yes. You'll be the best dressed woman there and the prettiest."

She giggled. His compliments were welcome change. "Now that you talked me into this, what sort of restaurant is it?"

"It's an Amish food restaurant."

She giggled as they both got into the car. "That's kind of obvious. I don't know why I didn't think it was. I had my mind fixed on something else."

"No. Just good old-fashioned Amish food."

"Good. I'm quite hungry. Which way?"

"To the left and follow that road into town."

As they drove, she was happy she hadn't stayed alone in the room. Once they were in the main street of town, he directed her down a back road.

"Here it is." He pointed to a building that was well lit, with people coming and going.

"Oh, it looks like a house."

"It once was. It's much bigger when you get inside."

They found a parking space nearby, and headed to the restaurant. When they walked in, the woman at the front greeted him by name and then a man called out and waved at him from across the room. When they walked further in, the aroma of the food greeted Selena's nostrils, it smelled like her home used to when she was a child.

Gabriel whispered to Selena, "That's Michael Glick, the owner."

Selena had a good look at him. He was a man of around forty and he seemed pleased to see Gabriel. He made his way over to them. "Gabe, what brings you out tonight?"

"Hunger mostly. Michael, this is Selena, a good friend of mine, and she's Abner Troyer's daughter."

"Granddaughter." She corrected him with a laugh.

"Yes. I'm sorry." He rubbed his chin.

Michael stared at her. "Really? You're Kate's daughter?"

"You know my mother?"

"I do. It's nice that you've come back."

"Find us a quiet table, would you, Michael?"

Michael looked around the restaurant. "It's gonna be hard tonight. How about there in the far corner?"

"Perfect."

They followed Michael to the table and he put a reserved sign on it. "You know the drill, when you're ready grab a plate and fill it."

Selena had already figured out it was an all-you-can-eat restaurant.

"*Denke*, Michael."

"Your meals are on the house tonight." Michael looked at Selena and smiled.

"Hey, you don't have to do that," Gabriel said.

"I told you before I owe you one." He gave Gabriel a slap on the back.

"Okay but that's not what I came here for. I had to feed Selena. She needed a decent meal. She's fading away to nothing."

Michael chuckled. "She looks fine to me. Anyway, enjoy yourselves."

"Thanks, Michael." Once he'd walked away, Selena said, "He seems nice."

"Everyone in the community's nice."

She smiled at him. "Why does he owe you one?"

"I sent a lot of people here when his business was getting off the ground. I guess that's what he means." After a waitress set down crusty warm rolls and butter for them, Gabriel asked, "Are you ready to get some food?"

"I sure am."

"After you."

She made her way to the serving counter and side-by-side they filled their plates with the familiar foods she'd missed. Her mother stopped cooking food like that when Frederick had died, back when Selena was a young teenager. Then they'd survived on takeout.

Selena filled her plate with roasted meat in gravy, mashed potatoes, buttered noodles and green beans until she couldn't fit any more on her plate. She glanced at Gabriel's plate to see he'd chosen the same. "We like the same food."

He looked at her plate and laughed. "It seems we do."

They headed back to their table, and Selena didn't waste time before she had a mouthful of the meat. It almost melted in her mouth. "Mmm. I didn't think I'd say this, but this is even better than my mother used to make."

He laughed at her. "I won't tell her that when I meet her."

"You'll never meet her. She'll never come here because she'd miss her soap operas on TV. They're on every day, and on the weekends she watches replays of them. She's addicted."

"She won't come to our wedding even?"

Selena laughed at him and shook her head.

Once they'd eaten and had both decided against dessert, they were still sitting at their table, when Gabriel suggest a walk before they went home.

"Yes, why not?" She found herself enjoying his company.

As THEY WALKED down the darkened road, Selena felt comfortable enough to share something with him. "Want to know a secret?"

"Sure."

"From the time I was a little girl, I was always fascinated by the Amish. I was upset with my mother for leaving. I told her she should've stayed on."

"Is that right?"

She looked up at him and saw his smiling face. "Yes. I begged her to sew me an Amish dress and *kapp* and she did. I used to wear them around the house." She giggled as she remembered the feeling she got while wearing them.

"Maybe you were right and she was never meant to leave."

She shrugged. It would've been difficult to stay considering the circumstances of her birth. "I was born out of the community. My life would be so different if she'd stayed."

"Better, I hope."

"I would've had no college degree, no police training, and I wouldn't have met Eugene."

"Yes, better."

She laughed at him. He was becoming so easy to be around now that she understood him a little better. With him, nothing was hidden because he always said what he thought without filtering it or worrying how others would react.

After they walked a few paces farther, he said, "I can show you my store. It's not far from here."

"Okay. I'd really like to see it."

They walked onto a busier road and then he stopped in front of a double storefront with large glass windows. The sign read, *Amish Crafts.*

"I don't have keys with me: otherwise I would've shown you inside."

"That's all right. I can get the idea what it's like from here. I didn't think it would be this big." She put her hands up and peered into the window looking at the small wooden toys, the quilts, the sewing kits for samplers, and all manner of Amish goods. "Wow, there's everything in there."

"I know. It does well."

She looked up at him. "You're so different from when I first met you. I have to tell you I thought you were a little ... well, loopy."

"Loopy?"

"Looney, um, well crazy. Not right in the head."

He threw his head back and laughed like he usually did. "Thanks very much."

"You thought God had sent me to marry you or something."

"That's right. Does that make me crazy?"

"Yes, kind of." She stared at him.

"I hope you don't still think that." He chuckled.

"Not now, but we're not getting married."

He ran a hand through his hair. "I can always hope, Selena. You can't take hope away."

Now it was her turn to laugh. "I'm getting married to Eugene and that's that. If you hope too much you'll end up disappointed."

"If you were my fiancé, I would've accompanied you on this trip. I'd always be with you."

"Ah, but he's a very busy and hugely successful lawyer."

"Hmm." He looked down at the ground. "That's too bad."

"No, it's good." When he didn't respond, she had to know what he was thinking. "What's bad?"

"I'm guessing he works long hours and that's why you're not happy?"

"Who said I wasn't happy?"

"I did."

"What makes you think that?"

His eyes twinkled. "You came out to dinner with me."

"Yes, but just as friends. It wasn't a date. I'm in love with my fiancé."

"Okay. I believe you." He kept walking and she caught up with him. "Have you been in love before?" he asked.

"Not before him, no. I've only had two boyfriends before him and only for a couple months at a time. They weren't long relationships."

"How do you know if it's real love with Eugene?"

"Because I couldn't imagine being with anyone else. And, I certainly wouldn't marry an Amish man." She giggled at the thought.

"Your whole family was Amish, so I don't think it's out of the question."

"It definitely is."

"That's sad. I guess we won't be getting married then."

"I'm glad you finally understand."

"As I said before, I can hope. With a woman like you, my life would be complete. I'd be a happy man for the rest of my days. There'd be nothing else I'd want apart from food and water, and a roof over my head."

She rubbed her chin, and looked up at him as his pace quickened. "Surely there's a woman in the community who'd suit you?"

"No, there are none, sadly."

She hurried to keep up, but it was hard in her heels. "Someone will come along."

"Perhaps."

"Can you slow down a little?"

"Oh, yes. I'm sorry. I usually walk that briskly. I was walking slower before so you would feel more comfortable. We should head back to the car."

"Okay." They turned back to the car, and she was surprised she didn't want the night to end. Surely she was just lonely because she was away from Eugene. When her cell phone rang, she fished it out of her bag and saw it was Eugene. She flipped the phone onto silent and let it fall from her fingers into her bag.

"Is that your ..."

"Yes. I'll call him back later."

"Don't mind me. Call him now if you'd like. I'll walk down the road a little and you can stay here."

"No, it's fine. It'll just go to voicemail and I'll call him back later." A few paces later, she asked, "Did you go on *rumspringa?*"

"No. I didn't feel the need. Most of my friends did. Two of them never came back. It's sad, really."

"Do you have brothers and sisters?"

"It's just me. What about yourself?"

"I'm an only child too."

"Ah."

"What do you mean?"

He looked at her. "What's that?"

"You said 'ah,' like there was something wrong with being an only child."

He laughed. "I'm one. I meant nothing by it. I just made a sound. It didn't mean anything. Relax. You're all wound up." He put his arms behind her neck and touched the top of her shoulders with both of his hands. "Yes. You're full of tension." He let go of her.

"You're right. I guess everything over the last few days has been a lot to process."

"That's true. It must be hard for you."

If he could see that why couldn't Eugene? Eugene couldn't see past his busy life to realize she had needs as well. What would it be like to have a relationship with a man like Gabriel? All his attention would be focused on her. It would be a welcome change.

Selena was sad the night was coming to an end and, seeing as the next day was Sunday, she knew she wouldn't see Gabriel again until Monday.

CHAPTER 21

AT THE END of the preaching on Sunday, the bishop made announcements.

"I'm sure many of you remember a few years ago when our friend and brother Abner was sent to prison for a crime?" Half the crowd nodded and murmured. "If anybody has any information about that, anything at all that you think might be important, please see me or Ettie Smith."

Elsa-May whispered to Ettie, "He wasn't supposed to say to see him."

"I know," Ettie whispered out of the side of her mouth.

"What use is that?"

"Shh."

When people turned around and stared at them, Ettie smiled back. The bishop continued with his announcements and then it was time for fellowship and the meal afterward.

Ettie was standing outside the house where the meeting had been hosted, hoping and waiting for someone to approach her, while Elsa-May helped herself to a meal.

"I have some information for you, Ettie."

Ettie turned around to see Gabriel's aunt, Ruth. "That's good. About whom?"

"We can't talk here. Can you come to my *haus* after the meeting?"

"*Jah*, I can do that."

"I have something to show you. Oh, you don't have a buggy, do you?"

"*Nee*. We don't. Jeremiah and Ava take us to and from the meetings."

"I'll take you to my place and then take you back to your home, okay?"

"That would be wonderful. I'll just tell Jeremiah that we don't need a ride today." As she looked around for Jeremiah or Ava, she saw both of them getting into their buggy. When she found Elsa-May, she learned what had happened.

"They've gone because she's going into labor," Elsa-May told her.

"Right now?"

"*Jah*."

"That's *wunderbaar*. Oh, and Ruth Yoder is taking us home, but before that she said she has something to show us at her *haus*. Something to do with Abner."

"Has anyone else talked to you?"

"*Nee*, that's all," Ettie said.

WHEN ETTIE and Elsa-May got to Ruth's house, she had them sit at the kitchen table and then she used a step-stool to get a box from on top of the kitchen cupboard. It was a cardboard box with floral paper glued onto it.

"These are things from Gabriel's mother. He said it was family papers and I would have more use of them." She carefully opened the lid and placed it beside the box. "I have a letter. It never made much sense but now I think it does." She took out a yellowed piece of paper, unfolded it and handed it to Ettie.

Ettie took the letter and read it. It was a letter to Gabriel. His mother apologized to him for having 'father unknown' on his birth certificate, and told him his real father was Wayne something; the last name was partially there but hard to read because it had been eaten through by moths. Ettie looked up at Ruth and handed the letter over to Elsa-May.

"I know the man who was run down was called Wayne. Do you think this might have anything to do with it? My *schweschder* was in and out of the community for a while, and she never told me who Gabriel's father really was."

Elsa-May adjusted her glasses and read the letter. "The same Wayne?" Elsa-May asked as she handed the letter back. Ruth absently refolded it and laid it in the box.

Ettie told Ruth, "We have been told that Wayne was involved with two Amish women. I wonder if it's the same Wayne. You never raised this issue with Gabriel?"

"*Nee*, he mustn't have gone through all the paperwork. I didn't want to upset him especially with no last name that is decipherable."

"It's not much of a clue," Elsa-May said. "There must be many *Englischers* named Wayne in the world."

"The time frame, though, Elsa-May."

"What do you think we should do with this information?" Elsa-May asked Ruth.

Ruth fetched the letter back out of the box. "You tell him."

Ettie's mouth dropped open. She recalled how Selena had taken the news about her father's identity.

Elsa-May leaned forward, took the letter, and rose to her feet. "We'll have to go there now, Ettie."

"Want to take my buggy? He doesn't live far away."

"Would you mind?" Elsa-May asked.

"If I'd minded I wouldn't have offered," Ruth said.

Ettie stood and followed Elsa-May out of the house, still not sure whether they should talk with Gabriel.

As the sisters approached the buggy, Elsa-May said, "You want to drive?"

"*Nee*, you do it."

Elsa-May climbed into the driver's seat and Ettie sat next to her. "It's been a long time since I've driven a buggy," Elsa-May said.

"I know, me too. How are we going to tell him? He'll be devastated."

"But we don't know for sure, Ettie. It's just telling him, which is showing him the letter and then he can go make his own conclusions."

Ettie shook her head. "Okay." Half of Ettie didn't want to tell him, the other half thought he should know.

"I can't believe Ruth's the only person who came up to you after the meeting with any information."

"Mmm-hmm. The only one out of everybody. No one went to the bishop. I kept an eye on him. Every little piece of information puts another piece of the puzzle together and pieces will solve the mystery."

"I hope so. I really can't say it will be to everyone's satisfaction, though."

When they pulled up at the house, Gabriel came out to meet them.

"This is an unexpected surprise. I've only just got home from the meeting."

"This is a letter from your Aunt Ruth," Elsa-May said, matter-of-factly.

He stared at them looking a little confused. "I just saw her today. Isn't that her horse and buggy?"

"*Jah*, she let us borrow it so we could talk with you. You see, the reason we are here is because … can we come inside, Gabriel?"

"Of course. Come into the living room."

Once they were sitting down, Elsa-May said, "Ruth gave us this letter out of the box that you gave her after your mother died." She passed it to him.

"It might be a little disturbing," Ettie told him as he stared at the letter in his hands.

He frowned at them, and after he read it the letter dropped into his lap. Looking up, he said, "My father's name was Wayne?"

"That's what it says." Elsa-May nodded.

"You don't think it's the same Wayne ..."

"It's a possibility," Ettie said. "The time frame fits."

Elsa-May said, "We can't rule it out since there was talk of him seeing two Amish women at the same time."

"I guess it makes sense. I'm not sure when she was in or out of the community. I just know she was in and out about the time of my birth. I guessed my father was an *Englischer*, that part was obvious, but she'd never talk about him. I was two when she returned and got baptized into the community and that's all I know."

"She never married even though there were several attempts to match her with men in the community, by nearly everybody," Elsa-May said.

"Yes, I heard there were a lot of people who tried to match her with potential husbands, but my mother just wasn't interested. I thought it was because she loved my father so much." He slowly shook his head. "Now I think the opposite was the case. It is possible she never trusted a man again because of what Wayne did to her. Did he abandon her? Cheat on her? It seems so, especially if we're talking about the same Wayne."

Ettie said, "I'm sorry to deliver the news to you like this, but we thought you should know because if this Wayne is your father, that means ..."

"Oh no ... that means that I might be closely related to Selena. I have to find her and tell her." He jumped up. "I'm sorry to leave in a rush like this."

"It's quite all right. We just came to give you the letter." Elsa-May and Ettie headed to their borrowed buggy while Gabriel headed to the barn to hitch up his own buggy.

CHAPTER 22

SELENA WAS TAKING the day to herself and reading in the garden area of the bed-and-breakfast. It was Sunday and her newly made Amish friends would be at their church gathering and wouldn't be able to help her that day. She was tired of all the wedding plans and she didn't want to think about her grandfather, her mother, or Wayne. Just as she was getting into the story, a deep voice came from behind her.

"Hello."

She jumped and looked around. "Hello. I wasn't expecting to see you today."

Gabriel took off his hat and smoothed his hair over to one side before he placed it back on his head. "I have received some rather distressing news. And I'm not sure if it's the truth or not."

"What is it?"

"I don't know if you know this, but my mother was raised Amish. She left and didn't fully commit to the Amish community until I was two."

"What does that matter? She got baptized into the Amish, didn't she?" He nodded and she laughed. "Why's that distressing?"

"Because I just learned, from a letter my mother wrote to me before her death, that my father's first name was Wayne."

Facts bombarded her mind. She knew they were the same age and Wayne was known to have been in a relationship with another Amish woman besides her mother. "It's a coincidence."

"Don't you see?"

"Oh! I do—you're saying we could be brother and sister?" Selena stared at him. It had been one thing after another and now this news was too much.

"Yes, that's the problem." He crouched down beside her. "Where do we go from here?"

"I have a friend in New York, Jake, who works in a laboratory testing DNA. I'll call him and see if we can both be tested to see if we are related."

"Will it give definite results?"

"Usually does, within 99.9%"

"Excellent, when can we do that?"

"Stay here. I've left my phone in my room. I'll call him right now."

She called her friend and a few minutes later, came back out to the garden. When Gabriel saw her, he jumped up from the chair. "What are you doing tomorrow?" she asked.

"Nothing that I know of."

"He's arranging for us to go to a laboratory. It's half an hour's drive away. He's got some friends there and he said he said he'll persuade them to perform the test on us."

He smiled. "Good. What does that involve? Not a needle, I hope."

"No. It's just a mouth swab."

He shrugged his shoulders. "That's good because I hate needles. And will they be able to tell us on the spot?"

"No, we'll find out the next day, or maybe later the same day. He said they'll rush everything through for us."

"You seem to know some pretty influential people."

"Not really. Maybe I know some useful people. I went to college with Jake and he went one way in his career and I went another. He's going to call me first thing in the morning and he'll give me a time to be there. So, I'll collect you some time tomorrow."

"Great. I'll be waiting." He sighed. "I didn't want to find out who my father was like this."

"We're only testing to see if we share the same father."

"You know your father is Wayne Robinson. Because your mother admitted it."

"That's right."

"My father could be anyone called Wayne. I always thought … well, I always hoped to meet him one day. I missed having a father. I was the only one who never had a father until a boy in the last year of school lost his father to an illness. The difference was that he knew his father and I never knew mine. He had his father with him and I just had a gaping hole. *Mamm* was good, but it was never the same, you know?"

"I can imagine it would've been awful. Everyone seems to have perfect families in the Amish community. Your mother was a brave woman to return and never marry. I imagine it would've been a lot easier for her to marry someone."

"Maybe," he said.

"It would be funny if we were siblings because we've always grown up as single children, the only child in the family and now we find each other like this."

He shook his head. "As nice as it would be to find I have a

half sibling, I don't want it to be you. It would be the worst thing in the world because we couldn't marry."

She smiled at him. He was still thinking they might marry if they weren't related.

When he left a few minutes later, she couldn't go back to relaxing and reading her book. She'd only had ten minutes of relaxation that day and since she'd arrived she'd had one surprise after another. She closed her book in her lap and looked out at the garden. Gabriel was growing on her somehow and she didn't want him to be related to her, either. If only Eugene could've been more like Gabriel. Gabriel didn't care what anyone thought about him and, in her eyes, that was an attractive trait. She pushed his looks out of her mind, in case he was her half-sibling. That's something she didn't need to be thinking about.

~

ELSA-MAY INSISTED on being the one to call Jeremiah to see if her great grandchild had arrived. She was told they'd been blessed with a boy. A very healthy and large baby boy of nine and a half pounds. She was assured Ava was doing well, too.

She hung up the receiver of the phone in the shanty and waited until Ettie caught up with her. "It's a boy."

"That's *wunderbaar.* When are we going to see him?"

"In a couple of days, I'd say."

"Okay. Ava will need to rest. Good idea. Have you called the taxi yet?"

"I'm just doing that now."

CHAPTER 23

When they got to the library, Ettie had a look to see what the Internet said before she headed to the microfiche to look through the newspapers. "It's here, Elsa-May."

"Quiet, Ettie. It's a library."

Ettie lowered her voice. "It says the robbers cut a hole through the bank's roof, cut the wires to the surveillance video and then they lowered themselves into the vault. When the bank employees came in the next morning, there were empty boxes scattered everywhere."

"What date?"

"The same year Wayne was run over. He was killed in August, the robbery happened in Florida, in April."

"It could be a coincidence and Florida is a distance away."

Ettie shook her head. "You know I don't believe in coincidences and Florida isn't too far to go to steal millions."

"See what else, Ettie."

She typed in Abner Troyer's name. His name stared at her from the screen in relation to him being held in jail for contempt of court for refusing to take an affirmation in place of the usual oath. Ettie relayed that information to Elsa-May.

"Oh, there's more. They mention Abner in connection to the robbery. It says here, *he was held on suspicion of running down Wayne Robinson,* and it gives the year he was run down, then it says, '*who was rumoured to be involved in the Florida bank heist where reportedly millions of dollars worth of goods were taken from safe-deposit boxes.*'

"It says Abner was involved?"

"*Nee*, Wayne, of course."

"I see. The way you read it, I thought you meant they thought Abner was involved. Shall we check the microfiche now?"

"*Nee*, I think that's all we need."

"Should we tell Kelly we know this?"

Ettie rubbed her chin. The police station wasn't far from the library. "Not just yet. Not until we piece a few more things together. We'll go home, and see what happens over the next couple of days. Kelly said he'd look into things and he might need our help sooner or later. Let him come to us."

WHEN SELENA and Gabriel arrived at the laboratory the next day, Selena and Gabriel met a man called Mike, who was a friend of Jake's. Mike said he might even have the results ready that afternoon. After they had their swabs taken, they headed back home with Selena sincerely hoping they'd have the results that day or she'd have another sleepless night. She knew Gabriel was equally anxious.

They stayed the remainder of the day talking in the garden of the bed-and-breakfast. When the results hadn't come by five o'clock, they guessed they weren't going to know that day.

"If they call me, I'll drive over and tell you immediately," Selena said.

"I should go home, or ... we could go out for dinner again ...?"

She shook her head. "I'll see you tomorrow. As soon as I know anything. Or, you could come back and join me for breakfast? If you want, I'll let Mrs. Williams know I have a guest coming for breakfast. I'm sure that'll be okay."

"Sure, I'd like that."

"Come at eight. It'll be better than you trying to cook for yourself. I've seen how that turns out."

He smiled at her, a little less animated than usual. "True. I'll look forward to it."

~

IT WAS after Selena and Gabriel had eaten breakfast together the next morning that Selena realized she'd left her cell phone in the room. She headed back there with Gabriel to see if she'd missed calls that might have been from her friend, Jake, or from the laboratory. Just as she unlocked the door, she heard her phone and made a lunge for it before it stopped ringing.

"Hi, Selena."

She recognized the voice as Jake's. "Hi. Heard anything yet?" She flipped the phone onto speaker, so Gabriel could hear. "Gabriel is here, too, so I'm putting you on speaker."

"Yes. The results are negative, so you are not closely related to your friend. You have similar DNA but that's not uncommon in groups like the Amish who have originated from a small group of people. Having said that, you don't share the same father. You aren't brother and sister and neither are you first cousins."

"Thanks so much, Jake, and tell Mike a big thank you for doing it so quickly."

"It was a pleasure. Anytime. I'll see you when you get home."

She ended the call and looked over at Gabriel. "You heard that?"

"I did. That's excellent news and now there's nothing stopping us from getting married."

She laughed it off. Before she was done laughing, a figure loomed in the doorway of her room. It was Eugene, her fiancé. Selena was immediately worried he might jump to conclusions with Gabriel having been in her room. She was thankful they'd left the door open.

Eugene looked Gabriel up and down and then looked at Selena. "Now I know why you didn't call."

She ran over to him and hugged him. "What are you doing here?"

"I had the chance to come here to interview a possible witness. Then I decided to come to them and see you on the way."

"I can't believe it. I missed you." He looked so good in his perfectly tailored dark blue suit, crisp white shirt and blue tie. His short-cropped hair was always the same and suited him.

He put his arm around her staring at Gabriel all the while, then said to her, "I missed you too."

Gabriel cleared his throat.

Selena said, "Oh, this is Gabriel."

Gabriel reached forward and shook his hand.

"Nice to meet you, Gabriel," Eugene said.

"Gabriel is the caretaker of my grandfather's house and we're just going over a few details."

"Ah, yes. I thought the name of the caretaker was John Yoder, isn't it?"

"That's right. I go by my middle name, Gabriel."

Eugene raised his eyebrows. "I just drove past the house and was surprised to see people living in it."

Selena nodded. "I was too, but then Gabriel explained about the upkeep and the costs. My grandfather didn't leave anything for that. I haven't had time to talk to you about it yet, but Gabriel has leased the place to pay for taxes and repairs, and things like that. I met the family and they are very nice."

Eugene nodded. "If you're okay with that then I am too."

"Well, I'll leave you two to talk." Gabriel nodded to both of them and then walked out the door.

Eugene closed the door behind him and then reached out with both arms and pulled Selena to himself. "I really have missed you, you know. And I'm sorry I've been uptight all the time."

"I understand the stresses of your work and everything."

"I know, but it's no excuse to be short with you."

After he stopped hugging her, she asked, "How long can you stay?"

"Only about an hour or so. Then I need to get to my appointment."

"Is that all? Just an hour?"

He glanced at his watch. "After I do my interview, I have to head back. The man lives half an hour from here on the way back."

"I wish you could stay a day or two. We haven't spent much time together for ages."

"I can't at the moment. As it is, I shouldn't have taken this time off to come here."

"How long did it take you to get here?"

"Nearly three hours with traffic. Are you looking after my car?"

"I am, only there's no way to keep it out of the weather here. It's just in the open parking lot."

"I saw that. I'm sure it'll survive the next couple of days. When are you coming back?"

"When I get the estimate from the realtor."

His mouth fell open. "Haven't you done that yet?"

She bit her lip. "No, I haven't."

Slowly he shook his head and gave her a disapproving glare. "What have you been doing here for the last few days?"

"I've been meeting with people my grandfather knew."

His gaze fell to the DNA paperwork on the small desk. "DNA?" He stared at her.

"Yes, I was just curious about my heritage."

He narrowed his eyes at her. "You know your heritage. Your mother and father were Amish, weren't they?"

"No. I've told you this before. My mother was raised Amish and left when she was eighteen and married my father who wasn't Amish." She could say that in all honesty because neither the man who raised her or her real father were Amish.

"Is something going on that you are not telling me about?" he asked.

"What do you mean?"

"You're acting kind of funny and so was your caretaker. Is he the reason you want to stay for a few extra days?"

She laughed. "Are you jealous?"

"No. You're right. It's silly of me to even think about being jealous of an Amish man like that. Well, would you care to come to lunch with us?"

"You said you only have half an hour."

"I can stretch that a little," he said.

"Um, I've only just had breakfast."

"We'll call it brunch, then."

She frowned. "Did you say 'us'?"

"Yes. Elga came with me. She's in the car."

"Oh, that's strange to bring her with you."

"She's my number-one secretary and besides, I needed her to share the driving on the way back so I can doze off."

"Oh, good idea. Sure, I'll come to brunch, but I can't say I'll eat anything." She pushed the DNA paperwork into her bag. "I'll just freshen up." She took her bag with the paperwork into the bathroom with her. It had her name on it and Gabriel's name, so she couldn't risk Eugene seeing it. She'd had a close call with that one.

When she came back out, he looked her up and down as he leaned on the small TV table. "Is that what you're wearing?"

She stared down at her casual clothes. There was no reason to wear anything else other than jeans, blouse and black pumps. She wasn't going for a job interview. "Yes, why?"

"Because this will be the first time Elga is meeting you."

"Does that matter? She's your secretary and we're not going to a Michelin-rated restaurant, are we? There are none around here anyway."

"No, but you know how appearance is important to me. She's got a picture in her mind of how beautiful you are because I tell her about you all the time. You fall short of my description in that. I'm sorry, but I've always said I'd be honest with you, didn't I?"

She licked her lips, wondering what to say. "I'm tired of your superficial world and you being so wound up in material possessions and ego-driven nonsense."

His mouth fell open. "Babe, where's this coming from?"

"And I hate it when you call me "Babe." I'm a grown woman with my own mind and I'll decide what I wear."

"You said you like it when I make all the decisions."

"I used to."

"Where's this coming from? Has that caretaker been putting ideas into your head?"

She stared at him and couldn't speak.

Through gritted teeth, he said, "Do you know how much time I've wasted coming out of my way to see you?"

"No, but I'm sure I'll hear about it more than once." She was grateful he'd taken the time to visit, but she also knew he would've been doing work in the back seat of the car while the secretary drove. She wondered if she was being a little unreasonable. "I'm sorry. It's just that everything's taking a toll on me."

Eugene breathed out heavily. "Is the wedding too much for you?"

"A little." She was just about to ask him if he could help with some of the decisions.

"I've got a good solution."

"What?"

"We forget about it. Or, we postpone it."

Her mouth fell open and she felt like all the air had been knocked from her. "Is that what you want to do?"

"You aren't you anymore, and I know it's got something to do with that DNA report and the man who was just here." He grabbed her bag, trying to open it, and she snatched it back.

"What are you doing?" she asked.

"Where are those papers?"

"They're none of your business."

"We're getting married, so I want to see who I'm marrying. What's going on? I want the truth. What have you found out?"

"I'm not saying."

"Something about your grandfather?"

She remained tight-lipped. If she told him she'd lose him anyway.

"This is not good enough. We're not married yet and you're already defying me."

"Defying you? I'm simply refusing for you to have a look at my paperwork. I didn't realize you wanted a Stepford wife, to obey your commands."

"This conversation is over."

"No, I'll say when it's over. My grandfather admitted to causing someone's death and ended up dying in jail. I've been trying to prove his innocence all this time." When his mouth fell open in shock, she was pretty sure it was all over.

"Your grandfather?"

"Yes, the one who left me the house."

He sat on the only chair in the room. "Tell me about him."

She sat on the bed and told him everything she knew, leaving out the part about who her father really was. "Do you think you could help?"

"That's what I do, Selena. I can't believe you didn't come to me with this."

"I thought you wouldn't want to marry me if you knew."

"Don't be ridiculous." He gave a low chuckle. "Now, what associations did your grandfather have with the man who was killed?"

"Just what I told you, Wayne worked for him now and again when something needed doing around the place."

"I'll tell you what. How about I stick around for a couple of days and help you with this?"

"Can you actually do that?"

He nodded.

"What about your cases?"

"I'll figure it out. This is important." He looked at his wristwatch. "I'll go to my appointment and then drive back, I'll send Elga back home in a rental car after our meeting's over."

"You'd really do that?"

He stood and walked to her. "Of course; we're getting married."

She stood and collapsed with relief into his open arms.

After a brief hug, he walked out the door. Her legs gave way beneath her and she sat on the bed drained of all energy.

Remembering Elga, she raced to the window and looked out. The woman she'd been so jealous of was not at all what she'd imagined. Elga was an elderly lady with her hair pulled back tightly and coiled into a bun. She'd imagined everything wrong about her and had been jealous over nothing. Then Eugene got into the car and the car zoomed away.

Selena waited until they had driven away and then got in her car and headed to Ettie and Elsa-May's house. This time, she was certain she knew the way.

CHAPTER 24

"Elsa-May, it's Selena come to visit us and she's by herself."

"Well, open the door. I'm knitting."

Ettie was knitting too, but she was glad to have a break from it. She left off in the middle of the row and jabbed the needles into the boring brown wool, and headed to open the door. "Hello, Selena."

"Hi, Ettie. I hope you two don't mind a visitor."

"We're delighted. We were just about to have a break. Care for a cup of hot tea?"

"I'd love one."

A few minutes later, they were sitting in the living room drinking tea. Snowy had been closed in Elsa-May's room as he got too excited with visitors until he got to know them better.

"I have good news," Selena announced.

"What is it?"

"I don't know if I mentioned it, but I'm engaged to a lawyer, and he's here. He can help us. He knows all the legal ins and outs. He might be able to prove my grandfather was innocent."

Elsa-May looked over the top of her knitting glasses. "You say he's here?"

"He's in town. He had some work to do, but he's coming back this afternoon."

"First of all," Ettie began, "congratulations."

Selena giggled. "Thank you. I never thought I'd marry someone like him. He's successful and he's got big career goals. He loaned me his car. He's very generous. I find that attractive in a man."

"Where did you meet him?"

"At a coffee shop I used to go to when I was off duty. Then we dated and we'd been dating for only three months when he proposed. It really was quite sudden, but I think things like that are romantic."

"I suppose when you know, you just know," Elsa-May said. "And did I remember you telling me you were only a police officer for a year?"

Selena smiled at her. "That's right. I was so upset about this whole family thing and my mother lying to me, but now, as soon as I saw Eugene, I wasn't quite so upset. Oh, and Gabriel and I took DNA tests and we aren't related. We don't have the same father."

"Oh, that is good," Elsa-May said.

"Yes." Ettie nodded. "Before Eugene gets back this afternoon, let's go through what we know so far."

"Okay."

Ettie said, "The case was unsolved and then when the detectives were re-investigating they came snooping around Abner's house because he had known the man. That's when he confessed."

"Why do you think he didn't do it?" Selena asked.

"We know him. He would've stopped to help the man if he'd accidently hit him, and he wouldn't have been driving a car in the first instance. He told the detectives he'd borrowed a friend's car, but wouldn't say which friend, why, or where he was going."

Elsa-May added, "We were looking into it and asking him a whole lot of questions, and then he died."

"Do you think he was killed?" Selena asked.

"No. He had a heart problem for the last few years of his life."

"Oh, I didn't know."

Ettie nodded. "When we visited him, he wouldn't talk to us about it. He always wanted to talk about other things."

"Ettie and I always thought he was protecting someone."

When Ettie saw Elsa-May give her a nod, she knew Elsa-May thought Selena should know about the other information they learned from the visit to the bar.

"There's something you don't know, Selena. We only just found out ourselves."

They told her what the man from the bar had said, and that they had confirmed it from what they learned at the library.

"Selena, why don't you bring your fiancé here for dinner tonight and we'll hash the whole thing out?"

"I'd love that. Thanks."

"And one more thing," Ettie said.

"Yes?"

"Does your fiancé know the whole truth about everything? Because I want tonight to be a night where the truth of everything is revealed. I've got other people I'll invite too."

"He doesn't know my father is Wayne, but I'll tell him before tonight."

WHEN SELENA LEFT, Ettie and Elsa-May realized they'd have

to go to the markets as they didn't have much in the larder, certainly not enough to feed all the other people Ettie wanted to invite. On the way there, they stopped by Ava's house to see the new baby boy, asking the driver to wait there for them. They had intended to wait longer to see him, but they couldn't.

As soon as Jeremiah opened the door of his house, Elsa-May pushed past him. "Where are Ava and the *boppli?*" she asked, already making her way toward their bedroom.

"In the bedroom," he called after them with a chuckle.

Ettie thought Elsa-May was being a little rude, but still she stayed close on her heels.

"Knock, knock," Elsa-May said when she reached the closed bedroom door.

"Come in," Ava called out.

Elsa-May pushed the door open. "How are you?"

"I'm fine. There he is in the crib, sleeping."

Ettie knew he wouldn't be sleeping long with Elsa-May and her booming voice in the room. Elsa-May walked over, leaned down and stared at the baby while Ettie sat on the edge of Ava's bed.

"He's a darling little *bu,*" Elsa-May said leaning over him.

"You'll give him a fright if he wakes up and sees you," Ettie said, which made Ava giggle. "And how was the birth?"

Ava sighed. "Good and bad. In a way, it wasn't as bad as some people said and in a way it was worse. I can't explain, but at least I know what to expect next time."

When Ava's mouth dropped open as she stared across to the other side of the room, Ettie turned to see Elsa-May holding the baby. "Elsa-May, he *was* sleeping!" Ettie said.

"He's still sleeping. I know what I'm doing, Ettie. I've had more *kinner,* and therefore more *grosskinner* and great *grosskinner* than you."

Ettie shook her head. "It's not a competition."

"If it were, I'd be the winner." Elsa-May cackled at her own words.

"It'll be my turn in a minute." Ettie turned back to Ava. "I'm sorry about her. At least he didn't wake."

Ava smiled. "I'm glad you've stopped by. What's happening with everything?"

"We don't want to worry you about anything just now. There is one point I want to clarify with Detective Kelly, and that's in regard to Frederick Lehman."

Ava shook her head. "If you told me about him it's left my head completely. Since I've been pregnant my mind hasn't been working properly."

"Let's hope you don't stay like that, like a certain other person." She nodded her head back toward Elsa-May.

"I heard that!"

"Don't wake him," Ettie said as she stood up to get a better look at the newborn. "He looks just like Jeremiah did as a *boppli.*"

"I was going to say that, but I knew you'd make a sarcastic remark if I had."

"Who me?" Ettie said.

"Jah."

"Put him back in the crib, Elsa-May. Let him sleep. I'll hold him another time."

Elsa-May gave him a soft kiss on his bald head and carefully placed him back in the crib. Then she walked over and hugged Ava. *"Denke,* for a beautiful great *grosskinner."*

Ava chuckled. "You're very welcome."

"Jah, they had him just for you," Ettie said.

Elsa-May turned toward Ettie and shook her head at her.

Jeremiah walked in. "What do you think about my *bu?"*

"He's the most beautiful *boppli* we've ever seen," Ettie said. Jeremiah chuckled. "We think so."

"We thought we'd be childless there for a while, but he showed up eventually. And, hopefully we'll have a few more," Ava said.

Ettie walked a few steps and kissed Ava on her forehead. "Of course, you will because Elsa-May wants more."

"He's lovely," Elsa-May said to Jeremiah ignoring her sister. "He looks just like you when you were that age."

Jeremiah smiled proudly.

"Jeremiah, would you fix us some hot tea and some of that cake Mrs. Langer brought over?" Ava asked.

"*Nee, denke,* we must keep going," Elsa-May said.

"We'll come back for a longer stay in a day or two."

Ettie and Elsa-May went back out to their taxi and continued on their way to speak with Detective Kelly.

"WE HAVE to be quick here. We've got so much to do before tonight." Ettie said to Elsa-May as they walked up the front steps of the police station.

"One thing I have to do quickly is use the bathroom."

Ettie giggled. They went their separate ways and Ettie spoke to Kelly once more.

"It's funny you should come here now because I've just learned an interesting fact. There were two Frederick Lehmans. One was employed in the government job, the other was unemployed and of no fixed address."

"Is that right? So, that means that you had the wrong facts when you were speaking to Selena about Frederick not being her father, but he wasn't. Hmm, that was a strange coincidence. What else have you learned?"

Ettie listened some more and then told him of her plans

for that evening. Then Elsa-May appeared at the door of Kelly's office.

"We have to go, Ettie. We've got so much to do."

Ettie pushed herself to her feet. "I'm coming."

"You're coming tonight?" Elsa-May asked Kelly.

"Of course he is," Ettie answered for him. "We can't chit chat all day, Elsa-May. Let's go." Ettie grabbed Elsa-May's arm and together they left the police station.

CHAPTER 25

IT WAS a rare that Ettie and Elsa-May had many people for dinner as their house was really too small for that sort of entertaining, but they'd managed to squeeze them in.

Even Jill James had agreed to come, and so had her brother, Terrence.

For the latter half of the day, Ettie and Elsa-May had been cooking together, but all along, Ettie had been thinking.

As people arrived, Ettie seated them in the living room until everyone was there. Several minutes later, their tiny home was full. Ettie had made sure to ask Selena if she minded Ettie revealing to everyone that she was Wayne's daughter, and she confirmed she didn't mind. *The truth has been hidden for long enough,* she'd said. Ettie was just about to announce that everyone could collect a plate and help themselves to the food when there was another knock on the door. She opened it to see Stacey. "Hello, Stacey." She was glad her neighbor was alone.

"I smelled something amazing coming from your house. I often smell your cooking at dinnertime and I'm so envious. Would I be rude if I invited myself to your dinner party?" She moved herself so she could better look around Ettie. Then she stared back at Ettie and fluttered her lashes while tilting her head to one side.

"Um, well, there are so many people here and you wouldn't know any of them."

"Are they all Amish?"

"No, only a couple of people are Amish. There is a girl whose mother used to be Amish and her fiancé, and then we have the detective, so I suppose you could join us if you'd like."

"A detective?"

"Yes."

"Why would you have a detective at your house?" Before Ettie could even start to answer, Stacey went on, "Greville said there was a detective at your house once and the detective was rude to him. I can't stay if it's the same one. I don't want anyone to be rude to me."

"It would be the same one."

She shook her head. "I won't be staying. You and Elsa-May should stop by maybe tomorrow. It would be good if you could do that before Greville is released from the hospital. You know how he doesn't like me having people to the house."

"How is he?"

"Better."

"Good."

Stacey turned and walked away. Ettie stared after her, wondering if she'd given the real reason for not wanting to be in close contact with a detective. She couldn't think about that now, she had too many other things on her mind. After closing the door, she turned and faced her guests. "Dinner is ready in the kitchen. Plates and cutlery are on the side. You can help yourselves and there are plenty of seats in the living room."

She hoped the dinner wasn't too cold since Stacey had delayed her.

AFTER EVERYONE HAD EATEN, Ettie cleared her throat. "Can I have everyone's attention?"

A hush fell over the gathering. "I've asked everyone here tonight so we can get to the bottom of what really happened to Wayne Robinson." She noticed Patricia looked annoyed. Perhaps she didn't care who had killed her cousin. "Selena, as you know by now, all the dates fit and we know that when Wayne was killed your mother would've been three months pregnant with you. She didn't meet the man who raised you until she was five months pregnant and married him a few weeks after you were born. Now, did she kill Wayne because he wouldn't take responsibility for his child?"

"She wouldn't have," Selena said.

"Or, Gabriel, did you read the letter you gave to your sister, Ruth, in that box with the other family papers? Did you do some research, or perhaps listened to Abner's stories, and think Wayne was your father?"

"I wasn't even born. I wouldn't have done it," Gabriel said.

"No, you didn't, but could someone close to your mother have taken vengeance on Wayne thinking your mother was having a relationship with him? He was known to be seeing two Amish women."

Gabriel shook his head. "No. It's not possible."

Ettie continued, "Patricia Langerfield." Ettie looked over at Patricia, who squirmed in her seat. "Not only did you think Wayne was stealing your alpacas, you were terrified of him. He cut the brake lines to your truck, causing a nasty accident—and he freely admitted to people he had done it. Something you didn't mention was that your father and Wayne's were brothers—making you first cousins."

"I was ashamed he was kinfolk," Patricia called out.

Jill James called out, "Well, he was ashamed of you." The two cousins glared at one another.

Ettie raised her hands, glad Patricia and Jill were on opposite sides of the small room. "Please, no arguments. The feud between you cousins goes way back to Wayne's side of the family being left out of the grandfather's will. Did Patricia do away with him to save her own life, thinking it was either her or him?"

"No, I didn't, but I probably should've." Patricia pouted her lips.

"Let's not forget someone who's so obvious, we've overlooked him, and that's Abner himself. What if he was guilty? He admitted to it, so perhaps he did it? Maybe he found out that Wayne was no friend and he'd gotten his daughter pregnant. Could Abner have borrowed a car like he'd said and gone to find Wayne simply to talk with him? Perhaps Wayne stepped onto the road and, filled with rage, Abner forgot everything else in his heart and mind and one thing was left —revenge. Or did Abner simply confess because he believed his daughter was the guilty party?" Ettie cleared her throat.

Elsa-May passed her a glass of water. "Have a sip."

"Thank you." Ettie took a mouthful and passed the glass back. "Selena, Frederick Lehman, the man who raised you as his own was being blackmailing by Wayne."

"Why?" someone called out.

"Good question." Ettie hesitated and continued pacing up and down.

Elsa-May leaned forward. "Are you going to answer the question this week?"

CHAPTER 26

Ettie looked at her sister, who wasn't knitting for once, as she sat in her usual chair surrounded by a sea of faces. "I'm gathering my thoughts." A deathly silence washed over the room. "Perhaps the guilty party and the one who killed Wayne is no longer with us—Frederick Lehman."

"No!" Selena called out. "He wouldn't have."

"You're right, Selena, the answer is no, and the only way you'd know that is if you've figured out the identity of the real killer."

Selena hung her head. "I don't have any idea."

Ettie continued, "Wayne was an opportunist. He wasn't only blackmailing his best friend over a robbery the friend had committed before turning from a life of crime, he was blackmailing his own brother."

Everyone turned and looked at Terrence. "I didn't do it, but, yes, he was blackmailing me. It's true."

"Terrence, you told me the world would be a better place without him. And, you told Abner that you knew for a fact that his daughter didn't do it."

"Abner's dead. Who told you that?"

"I did," Gabriel said. "I never had a father or a grandfather, and to me, Abner was like both of those in one. We'd sit by the fire and he'd tell me stories. He told me everything he remembered about the time leading up to Wayne's death and after it. I knew he didn't do it, and I knew he thought his daughter did." He looked at Selena. "I'm sorry. I couldn't tell you he thought that."

"That's okay. You didn't know for certain if she did it or not. There was really nothing to tell."

Gabriel continued, "Abner told me Terrence assured him his daughter didn't do it."

Everyone looked at Terrence, Wayne's brother. "Why would I do that? How would I know who did it or who didn't?" Terrence asked.

"Because you killed your brother," Ettie said. "Your car was given a speeding ticket minutes after the incident, and you were traveling north away from the scene of the crime."

"I get a lot of speeding fines. I've gotten many over the years. That doesn't mean nothing."

"The officer who gave you the ticket made notes about you having a broken headlight and various scratches on your car."

"This is where I take over, Mrs. Smith." Kelly stood up. "At the scene of the crime, headlight glass was found. We ran tests and found that it matched the same model car you owned at the time. The day after that, you disposed of that car."

"So what?"

"I'm glad you asked. We'll let a jury decide 'so what' because that information was enough for me to get a judge to sign off on a warrant for your arrest. Terrence Robinson, I'm arresting you for the murder of your brother, Wayne Robinson. Would you stand up please?" Kelly took handcuffs out of his pocket. "You have the right to—"

The man jumped to his feet, kicked his foot free from his plaster cast and made a run for it, leaving Kelly standing there as he fled out the front door with one foot bare.

"He won't get far," Kelly said. "I've got officers waiting for him outside." He chuckled as he leaned over and picked up the cast. "Looks like we'll look into insurance fraud to add to his list. He never had a bad leg from the look of his sprinting action."

Ettie pushed people out of the way, and hurried to the window to see two officers either side of Terrence, escorting him to a police car.

"Good work, Detective Kelly," Elsa-May said.

"Yes, I knew it would all come down to the car."

"Why didn't the people investigating the case come up with this information years ago?" Selena asked. "Then my grandfather wouldn't have had to die in jail."

"The technology for the testing on the glass wasn't around back then, and the second time we investigated, Abner confessed before it went further. When someone confesses, we don't keep investigating."

Selena nodded. "No, of course not."

Ettie looked at Eugene. "How did you meet Selena?"

He smiled. "We met at a coffee shop. It was one where we both used to go. I saw her there a few times and we struck up a conversation."

"How often did you go there before you talked with Selena?"

"A few times?"

Ettie stared at him. "Three, or four?"

He frowned. "Why do you ask?"

"I'm just trying to work out how much effort you put into all this."

"Ettie, what are you talking about?" Selena asked.

"Will you tell her, young man, or shall I?"

"I've got no idea what you're talking about." Eugene stood. "Let's go, Selena."

Selena hurried over to Ettie. "What is it, Ettie? What do you know?"

"Your fiancé here, read about the robbery Wayne was said to be involved with and it's my guess he was marrying you to get closer to the money. It would go a long way toward paying those student debts wouldn't it, Eugene? It must take a lot of money to keep up with your rich friends when you're on half their salary. How many cars are you leasing?"

"Leasing?" Selena stared at Eugene. "Half their salary?"

"She's mad. This old lady doesn't know what she's talking about. No one would work for half the money. Forget her."

Selena looked back at Eugene. "What's going on? I can tell when you're lying."

"Okay. I knew about the robbery and knew about Wayne, but that doesn't affect how I feel about you."

"You knew? Before you met me?"

"Yes, but she's talking complete rubbish about my salary. You've seen how much I get paid."

Selena's mouth fell open. "Did you follow me and deliberately meet me in the coffee shop?"

"I went there for coffee and saw you and wanted to get to know you better. It's not a crime. Okay, I'll tell the truth. I read about your grandfather, refusing to give an affirmation and swear an oath. I was fascinated, and then looked further into the man he was supposed to have run over, because I doubted he had done it. Then I read about the robbery. I've always loved bank robbery movies and here I'd found one in real life."

She held her head in her hands. "Everything is a lie." Looking up at him, she asked, "You knew about Wayne and the robbery and you sought me out. Why?"

Elsa-May said, "Because it seems like the man who raised you might have known about it too."

Eugene took a step toward the door. "This is a waste of my time. Are you coming, Selena? We'll go back home tonight and I'll send someone for the other car."

She shook her head. "No. I need to sort some things out."

"All right. You sort out your business and I'll see you when you get home." He leaned down to kiss her and she pulled away. Then he walked out looking angry and embarrassed.

There was silence in the room and Selena sat down feeling like a fool. She'd been oblivious to all the secrets and lies that had surrounded her from even before she was born. "That explains why he was so friendly with my mother and always asking questions about Frederick and his life. Frederick told me he did some bad things as a young adult, and then made amends and changed his ways."

Elsa-May stood and said, "We have dessert if anyone's still hungry. Any takers?"

"Yes, me." Jill James bounded to her feet.

Elsa-May stared at her. "Aren't you concerned your brother was just arrested?"

"No. It serves him right. We never got along. I was closer to Wayne except for that thing with the dog."

Elsa-May took people into the kitchen for the dessert, while Ettie stayed in the living room with Selena and Gabriel.

"Are you okay, Selena?" Gabriel asked crouching down next to her.

She shook her head. "I'm not. Everyone close to me has lied to me. My mother, the man I thought was my father, and my fiancé. If Wayne was my father like I've been told, my uncle is going to jail for killing him. It's going to take me a while to feel okay about anything."

Gabriel sat down next to her. "I'm sorry this has all happened to you."

"My fiancé is a fraud. I can't marry him, not now. He was just on some kind of a treasure hunt. He probably never would've gone through with the wedding. He only paid the wedding planner the deposit, and she kept asking about the final payment, so that kind of proves it."

"You still have me. I'll marry you."

Selena laughed. "I wonder what happened to the money." She looked up at Ettie who was standing nearby.

"I have no idea. Maybe Wayne hid it somewhere and his secret died with him, but if that was so, he wouldn't have needed to blackmail anyone."

Selena shrugged her shoulders. "My parents never had any money."

Ettie said, "Maybe Detective Kelly will find out more from Terrence."

"Do you want me to drive you back to the bed-and-breakfast, Selena?"

"Yes, I do. Thank you."

Selena said goodbye to the elderly sisters and left with Gabriel.

LATER ON, when everyone had gone, Elsa-May and Ettie were washing up.

"Ettie, something doesn't add up in my mind."

"Jah?"

"Didn't Kelly say Frederick Lehman was working in New York? How would he have done the robbery, which I remember was on a Tuesday night and get back in time for work the next day? It would've taken them all night to make that hole in the roof."

"Ah. Remember when you went to the bathroom in the middle of us talking to Kelly today at the station?"

"*Jah.*"

"That's when he told me, he had a closer look at Frederick Lehman and found it was another Frederick Lehman. Someone with the same name."

"Oh. It would've been nice if you'd told me that."

Ettie chortled. "There's been so much going on. I'm sorry, I forgot."

"Hmm, okay. I suppose I'll have to accept your apology." Elsa-May put the first of the dishes in the sink, while Ettie wrapped the leftover food. "I feel sorry for Selena. Do you really think that man would've married her for a chance at some money that had disappeared?"

"That's a good question and I have no idea of the answer. I'd love to know what happened to the money. Selena said her parents had next to nothing, and Wayne lived like a pauper according to Kelly."

"We'll have to find out."

"You know what else was funny?"

"What?"

"Frederick could've met Selena's mother here and they traveled to New York together. And you got suspicious because of the dates that Wayne was the father, and from Kelly's error about the mix up with two Frederick Lehmans, thinking Frederick was in New York at the time Selena was conceived."

"It was all a big mix up if you ask me. But, Selena's mother admitted Wayne was the father. My guess is that Frederick loved her from afar and didn't like the way Wayne treated her. One day Frederick made his move and revealed his feelings, then they ran away together after Frederick swore he'd go straight. Then they made a life together, a life that didn't include Wayne."

Ettie raised a bony finger in the air. "Ah, yes, that was their plan but right before they left, Wayne was killed."

Elsa-May chuckled. "History is repeating itself."

"What do you mean?"

"Look at Gabriel and that lawyer. The lawyer didn't treat Selena well, from what I can see and from the way he spoke to her, and there's Gabriel, obviously head over heels with Selena and ready to whisk her away."

Ettie chuckled. "You're right. We'll have to wait and see what happens there."

CHAPTER 27

IT WAS two days later when they saw Selena next. She sat down in the elderly sisters' living room with them. "I want to thank you both for all your wonderful help with all this."

"It was our pleasure. When do you go back?" Elsa-May asked.

"This afternoon, but I'm moving back permanently."

"Back here?" Ettie asked.

"Yes. I'll be staying in temporary accommodation and when the Kings' find somewhere else to live that they're happy with, I'll move into my grandfather's house. Of course, I won't own it until I'm thirty."

"Or until you get married, we're told," Elsa-May said.

"That's right. I'm going to make a life here. It's quieter and I prefer a peaceful life. I'm going to take some time to work out what I want to do with my life."

Ettie leaned forward. "And, does a certain man factor into your decisions?"

"Oh no. I've ended things with Eugene."

"Ettie meant Gabriel."

Selena's face flushed beet-red. "Oh, we'll see."

"He's extremely fond of you."

Selena nodded. "I know."

"Your mother will miss you."

"I'm not so sure. She's pulled herself out of her usual rut and she's going on a 'round the world tour."

"Really?"

Selena nodded.

"I thought you said your parents didn't have much," Ettie said.

"She won it in a competition."

"What competition was that?" Ettie asked.

She shook her head. "I'm not entirely sure, but she'll be gone for a good six months."

Ettie and Elsa-May looked at one another and each knew what the other thought. They'd just discovered what happened to the missing money. Of course, Frederick and Selena's mother would have needed to lay low for a while before they started spending it. Now, twenty-five years later, Frederick was gone and Kate decided it was a perfect time to start spending all those millions.

"I do hope you'll visit us when you get back," Ettie said.

"I will for certain."

"Will you have coffee and cake with us? We were just about to put the teakettle on," said Elsa-May.

"No thank you. I'm just about to hit the road back to New York. Then, when I settle everything up and my apartment is sub-let I'll come back here." She stood and gave each lady a hug, and then they walked her to the door.

"Still got your fiance's car?"

"Yes. I have to see him one last time when I return it." Her mouth turned down at the corners. "That'll be awkward." Selena gave them one last smile and got in the car and zoomed away.

Ettie and Elsa-May stood there waving to her until the car disappeared.

SELENA GOT out onto the open road and went as fast as the speed limit would allow. She finally felt free. Free of all the lies she'd been told throughout her life. How things had changed in the short time she'd visited Lancaster County. She'd found out her father wasn't her father, and that her newly found uncle had killed her newly-found-out-about father. Her mother had pulled herself away from daytime-TV to go on a world tour. Eugene was in her life no more, and she'd found a new love interest.

Giggling aloud, Selena's mind traveled to Gabriel—his handsome face and his unusual dark eyes. He was a strange man, but she found, not entirely to her dismay, that she was attracted to him and it wasn't just his looks.

Gabriel was kind, genuine and gentle, and he was what had been missing in her life. With him, she could be herself. But, for their relationship to go further she would have to join the Amish community. The prospect of doing so was daunting but also exciting. She hadn't mentioned it to Gabriel, but it was something she was seriously considering. When she moved to Lancaster County, she intended to look into it. She'd made some good friends and people like that were hard to come by.

"WELL, WELL, WELL," Elsa-May said as she closed the front door. "Frederick said he was going straight."

"Jah, easy to do when you have a few million stashed somewhere. I'm curious what Detective Kelly would think about Kate's trip. I wonder if he knows."

Elsa-May sat back in her chair and picked up her knitting. "And, I have a feeling that Gabriel has got a lot to do with her moving back here."

"So do I, Elsa-May, so do I."

"God has a plan for everyone, and it seems like His plan for Selena brought her here."

Ettie sat down in her seat by the window. Maybe today would be the day Greville came back from the hospital. "Weren't you going to put the teakettle on? You told Selena you were just about to."

Elsa-May grunted. "I've only just sat down."

"What would *Dat* say about you telling a lie?"

Elsa-May blew out a deep breath, and then pushed herself to her feet, while Ettie picked up the boring brown knitting and gave a private little chuckle.

∼

Thank your reading Amish Mystery: Plain Secrets.
I do hope you enjoyed it.
Samantha Price

If you'd like to receive my new release alerts, and special offers, go to www.samanthapriceauthor.com and add your email under the 'mailing list' section.

ABOUT THE AUTHOR

Samantha Price is a best selling author who knew she wanted to become a writer at the age of seven, while her grandmother read to her Peter Rabbit in the sun room. Though the adventures of Peter and his sisters Flopsy, Mopsy, and Cotton-tail started Samantha on her creative journey, it is now her love of Amish culture that inspires her to write. Her writing is clean and wholesome, with more than a dash of sweetness. Though she has penned over eighty Amish Romance and Amish Mystery books, Samantha is just as in love today with exploring the spiritual and emotional journeys of her characters as she was the day she first put pen to paper. Samantha lives in a quaint Victorian cottage with three rambunctious dogs.

www.samanthapriceauthor.com
samanthaprice333@gmail.com
www.facebook.com/SamanthaPriceAuthor
Follow Samantha Price on BookBub
Twitter @ AmishRomance

ANGST!
TEEN VERSES FROM THE EDGE

ANGST!

TEEN VERSES FROM THE EDGE

Edited by Karen Tom and Kiki
Illustrations by Matt Frost

Workman Publishing, New York

The Cataloging-in-Publication Data for this book may be obtained
from the Library of Congress.

ISBN 0-7611-2383-0

Workman books are available at special discounts when purchased
in bulk for premiums and sales promotions as well as for fund-rais-
ing or educational use. Special editions or book excerpts can be created to specification. For details, please contact the Special Sales
Director at the address below.

Workman Publishing Company, Inc.
708 Broadway
New York, NY 10003-9555

www.workman.com

Cover and book design by Matt Frost

Manufactured in the United States of America
First Printing, April 2001

10 9 8 7 6 5 4 3 2 1

3 wacky cats, closets full of clothes, cable TV
She's a luxurious gal, cool with a capital C
Brimming with class, and a brain to boot
Special thanks to Elaine—you're such a hoot!

CONTENTS

READ ME

In ancient Greek times, poets were considered the mortal beings closest to the gods. Today, things have changed. Gone is the Golden Age when society praised poets for passing along the traditions, emotions, thoughts, and history of the human struggle. Gone is the age in which poetry was considered the quintessential language for understanding the deeper meaning of life. Although we still revere the classical poets of ancient Western and Eastern civilizations, contemporary poets are not given the same glory as the ones long dead and disintegrated. So why be a poet or care about poetry now?

Honey, poets make the world go round! With a thriving number of followers, poetry's renaissance has arrived! As the perfect platform for those wishing to challenge the madness known as "Reality," poetry provides a powerful outlet in which to voice solutions for improving the world, expose new perspectives, share emotions, bond, or add fun and laughter. The poets of today are idealists, romantics, activists, artists, believers, anarchists, and nihilists. They all trust that despite the misery or boredom that can surround the day-to-day, there are still reasons to pursue poetry's inspirations and expressive language, and to share it all. Without these people, there would be nothing but the regimented world of "Produce and Acquire," and this place would absolutely suck.

Doing its part to save the world is *ANGST!*, a rock 'em—sock 'em poetry anthology from the impassioned young gals of PlanetKiki.com. Banding together from various corners of the globe, they remind us of the power, wisdom, and peace to be found in poetry. Through their raw and fearless voices—preserved in their original form—they reiterate the importance of questioning and responding to this saga known as life. Their words tell us that being open and honest is the only way to truly grow ourselves/our spirits. By showing us that it is in vogue to care, that silent apathy should not be an option, they remind us that it feels good to be a poet, and to bond with poetry.

After all, life is poetry. It's in everything we see, feel, taste, smell, and touch. It is in us, around us, and can be channeled through us. It's an expression of our pain, humor, anger, joy, lust, ennui, or any other of our infinite emotions. Poetry helps us understand and appreciate every detail of our daily existence—in all its torture and ecstasy. Poetry not only helps us grasp being alive; it is everything that makes us alive.

As for who and what PlanetKiki is all about, we are: Kiki, Karen Tom, Matt Frost, and a plethora of young girls dedicated to winning the revolution against tedium and absolute apathy. We aim to establish a new perspective devoted to the splendors of sharing all the thrills and chills of life. PlanetKiki.com is a home away from home, where anyone can join in and celebrate the liberation found in creative self-expression. Having spent three years growing in size and strength, we now present ourselves to the world through *ANGST!*—our map back to the Golden Age.

—Karen & Kiki

CHAPTER 1
SOCIETY'S ILLS

ETIQUETTE OF DREAMS

Why is it so hard to be a teenager?
Supposedly, these are the best years of life
If this is the best I can get
Well, I'm screwed
I want to be a REBEL WITHOUT A CAUSE
I want to break all the rules
Just to say I did
I want EVERYONE to know
I AM NOT AFRAID
I want to run away, and be on my own
Live on my own
Take care of all my wants and needs
Not what others want and need from me

Why does society try to impose
Its goals and expectations on me??
What about what I want to do with my life?
It is mine, isn't it?
Think about it . . .
How many of your goals are actually yours?
What do YOU want to do when you "grow up"?
Who knows better than you?

I confuse myself to no end . . .
So, how can everyone else tell me
What is best for me?
Do they actually know?

By telling me what I HAVE to
Accomplish,
They're pushing me closer and
Closer to the edge
One of these days, I just might
"Take the Plunge."

I want to break out of
SOCIETY'S RULES
Why must there be an
"Etiquette of Dreams"?
The dos and don'ts to
Childhood fantasy
Why do others tell me
What my definition of success should be?
What if I don't want money
Or a big house
Or a stable job in CORPORATE AMERICA???
What if I want to be
A rebel
A wanderer
Or a mysterious vagrant
Who travels with the world on her shoulders?
I may not want what others want,
But at least I know one thing,
I will not let others tell me what my dreams should be!

—MYRITA CRAIG

3

MULTIRACIAL IN A SMALL TOWN

don't laugh
at my plaid skin
while yours
white wonder
is so pure and clean
and your scorn
is like knives
in my multicolored back
piercing hot pain
in my heart
you make me dance
shoot at my feet
see the blood
it's red, like yours
but still you laugh
while my black hair
sways
and my tears fall
but peroxide will never befriend me
and I don't care about khaki clothes
you won't get me

4

white-bread wonder people
you won't catch me
because my eyes, they're smaller
and my hair, it's blacker
my clothes aren't all-American
and my skin is like olives
yeah, the ones you eat
I'll never be blue and blonde and white
all over
so laugh, and point, and shout
but you can never change me
while your white shutters
close on me
and you sprinkle rain on me
and your dog, it growls
and your mama calls the police
when all I want you to do
is come out and play

—BETHANN CLEARY

MODERN WOMAN

modern woman
painfully thin, and thinly skinned

starved of the fiber
present in a rich
and deep existence
subsisting on the sawdust
of society's agent orange
heavy enough to sit in her stomach,
make her full (empty),
and rough enough to give her shivers

leashed by the American dream
leashed in her American jeans

accenting every curve
conscious of every ripple
she steps cautiously,
swaying uncertainly
she searches for her swagger
two-inch tube top
left breast
lolling loose
casually

just like the magazine
just like Miss Teen Beauty Queen

pubescent, brace-faced, nascent child
what do you want from life?

—No, I am a woman—
indignantly, she expostulates
in anticipation of a change
impeded
amid the litter of pills and diet miracles
she pushes impatiently for her turn
 painfully modern.

—HANNAH RICHARDS

THE WHININGS OF A
LOWER-MIDDLE CLASS WHITE GIRL

you're bitter
because I have money
from my parents
with their credit cards
bitter because
if I'm hungry—I eat
and if I'm cold,
I put on more clothing,
or go inside

because I can afford
to buy the stupid crap
it took you decades and
seconds to learn and make
because in all this,
I disrespect my parents
and in all this,
I think I am without.

yes, you see,
I am bitter too.
I am bitter
like the rest of my sort—
because my hips are too wide
and because
I don't have enough friends
or that one special person

yes, because I won't
be valedictorian
and also because
my parents divorced . . .
  and remarried.
because I look at myself
and see something ugly
and no one else
has told me different

bitter
to the core
because I am
a stupid, sheltered
American tourist,
and we all want more
than what we have
or maybe it's just me
but goddamn,
do I wish I could
forget this adolescent nonsense.

—AMBER NICOLE LUPIN

LITTLE ORANGE FRIENDS

My little orange friends
They swim around their own waste
I feel like I swim with them
My life is like their dirty water
So unclear, and full of disgust
Their gills taking in the smelly oxygen
Just like I suck up the world's filth
They don't seem to mind what's going around
They seem content and wise
They love each other, more than they love themselves
Why can't we be more like them?
My little orange friends

—LIBBY GUNTER

THE FREAK'S THOUGHTS

I am a Freak with an open mind on life.
I wonder why people judge books by their cover.
I hear the voices of famous singers.
I see the stage lights flashing in my eyes.
I am a Freak with an open mind on life.

I pretend that I am famous.
I feel that God is fake.
I touch the souls of unforgiving people.
I worry that some things will never change.
I cry that my parents don't understand me.
I am a Freak with an open mind on life.

I understand that life is a roller coaster.
I say what I believe in.
I dream of a world that understands.
I try to love those I hate.
I hope that my friends will stay true.
I am a Freak with an open mind on life.

—SARAH STON

THE ROCK REVOLUTION

I saw the beauty in the heart of the song
Though I was 8, it didn't take me long
The sound just pounded through my veins
It was louder than the hardest rains
Some of you, you felt the same
The love, hatred and the pain
Now you all just see the faces
The little boy dance paces

Get that crap away from me
They aren't the ones I want to see
No-talent losers, you white-trash skank
I wish I could make you walk the plank

Now this really is going too far
The sounds of rock are hidden under the scar
Still pounding, taking over my soul
As the money-thirsty losers dig deeper in the hole
You know you all feel the same
Yet you listen to that pop that causes the pain
To those who have worked to earn their position
They are thrown in the gutter, for no one to listen

Get that crap away from me
They aren't the ones I want to see
No-talent losers, you white-trash skank
I wish I could make you walk the plank

Well, my friend, the end is near
The Rock Revolution is what you should fear
We'll lead the way, and they'll take over
Even if we seem like a 3-leaf clover
We'll get you back, you piece of trash
Take over those who just want your cash
You'll see who's the boss once more
The Rock Revolution, to the you, from the core

Get that crap away from me
They aren't the ones I want to see
No-talent losers, you white-trash skank
I wish I could make you walk the plank

—SARAH D. BOLAM

PLAYERS

Players collect hearts
to achieve their goal
the more they get
the less they care about what
    they've stole'

To date a player
is to go through so much pain
it's a hurt and a want of knowing
that's hard to explain

You know before you get into it
what will happen at the end
your heart will get torn apart
and the pieces will be hard to mend

But at the time it is so right
the closeness of his touch
and he holds you oh so tight
you could only dream of such

You're not the only one
or nearly the first
it's a desire, a craving
simply a thirst

You know as you're with him
he's playing on the side
for in days to come
there'll be many others in his ride

He wants your heart
with nothing in return
you know it's not right
but your heart simply yearns

He is so desirable
you almost drop to your knees
it seems he's so perfect
always striving to please

You want this dream world
this fantastical place
your heart melts before him
and your pulse seems to race

You're there, and he knows it
seductively trapped
this is what he planned to happen
he had it all perfectly mapped

(continued)

15

You give him your heart
and you know you've lost
this is the price you pay
love, at the highest cost

You pray it won't break
as he bends and twists it
he plays you like a fiddle
before he decides to take it

He puts it with the others
so carelessly placed
and this is the reality
with which you are faced

Part of you is gone
with him forever
and you swore to yourself
that he'd hurt you never

He's gone with you
gone the next day
it's over, you're done with
there's nothing to say

You pray that he'll hurt
and feel the same
but you know in your heart
he feels no pain

If you see him again
he won't even say hi
and it'll kill you inside
your tears will run dry

You'll think of him
for years to come
of the game you played
and wished you had won

Don't think you can win
the player's game
for once you have lost
you're never the same

—JEANA MITCHELL

PARTY

Party people, party faces,
    forget the pain within
Swirling drinks, laughing people,
    the room begins to spin
A half-eaten lime, a lipstick-stained glass,
    a twirling fun-filled world
A can of beer, a good mixed drink,
    it's the same, boy or girl
The party swells, the night rolls on,
    the usual personality changes
An empty cup, a dancing girl,
    a fleeting moment of fame
The glasses are empty, the party dies down,
    the tires begin to squeal
The gravel flies, the feelings soar,
    the party goes faster on wheels

The missed stop sign, a passing van,
  the horror of the night revealed
A broken horn, the smoke-filled air,
  the blood on a cracked windshield
A gruesome scene, the fading sun,
  a piercing pain within
A grieving mother, a dark somber funeral,
  and a child's small coffin
Crying hearts, blank sad faces,
  a mournful song in each ear
All this pain, all this sorrow,
  all for a tall glass of beer
So, before you party, before you chug,
  before you go to town
Remember my rhyme, and imagine yourself
  In that cold dark ground

—MABYN E. LUDKE

DON'T SCREW UP

Being a kid
It always sucks
You can't do anything
Can't even make 2 bucks!

You have no money
Have to do what you're told
Must give in easy
No treasure to hold

Soon you become a teenager
Wish to lurk at nights
But parents don't approve
They don't give you your rights!

All your friends
Passed around the booze
You know what's right
But which do you choose?

So you got drunk
Booze from then is a need
You think you've got it all
'Til someone passed around the weed

So you took that joint
Got high and wild
What was the point?
You're a child!

You've made bad choices
You've screwed up large
Usually Mom and Dad are wise
But now you're on your own, in charge

No home for the night
You look back some years
The idea to be out all night was bright
But now you're on the verge of tears

So don't screw up
Don't get high
Don't bother getting drunk
Believe me, you don't wanna die!

Bright future was ahead
Now you want that
But it's a million times as hard
When you don't have enough for bread

—DRAGANA N. BIJEDIĆ

21

SMOKING

It reels you in
Like a fish on a hook
It's hard to get away
Just like a good book

It gives you cancer
Bad breath and smelly hair
So why do it?
You should give your body care

Look at the people
Who choose to do this
They don't look happy
They look like piss

It kills and destroys
And makes you look bad
So, choose not to do it
And you will be glad

—JENNIFER BREWSTER

RUMORS

People I've never seen before
Go around and talk
Spreading these horrible words
Everywhere they walk
I hear them, and wonder
What did I do so wrong?
To make these people hate me
And call me words so strong
I don't deserve to be called a slut
I'm not a bitch
And I'm not a ho
Obviously people just don't care
And don't take this time to know
They only see this person
Through everyone else's lies
But they won't take the time
To look at me
With their own eyes

—ERICA SUTHERLAND

DON'T THINK SO

Tall
Blonde hair
Blue eyes
Every guy's dream, right?
Wrong.
I could have been a cheerleader
Jumping around in a short skirt
Throwing my hair about
I'd have guys' attention
But would that really be me?
Nah.
How about being on the basketball or softball teams?
Able to outrun a track star
Then, I'd have the jocks after me
I'd be in heaven
Don't think so.
Nope, I'm just me
Tall
Blonde hair
Blue eyes
A musician, a writer
Kinda smart, but not so quick
Always in thought, and writing a verse to tell
Will guys like me now?
Don't think so.

—JESSICA J. RATLIFF

PERFECT

Supermodel
Superway
Fix the mold
Don't break away
Perfect in the magazines
Perfect in your little dreams
Careful angel
Don't fall down
Fragile doll
Who's tied and bound
Perfect when you are 17
Perfect, so it seems
Plastic smile
Glossy eyes
No emotions, nothing to hide
Perfect in this scene
Perfect as your parents' beam
Honeysuckle
Babydoll
With your picture on my wall
You are everything I hate to see
You are everything I want to be

—KARI MYERS

WHO ARE YOU?

I am me,
Who are you?

Look in a mirror.

I see myself,
Brown & true . . .

You hide behind your compact,
Which is sinister & blue.

A cheerleader I am not,
But at least my body will not rot.

From all the impurities you put
Into your athletic body.

Why?

You smoke, drink, nearly kill yourself,
Because you want to fit in the crowd.

At your funeral, they'll look up at a cloud and
Say, "If only we had encouraged her individuality..."

You say I am lying, that situation won't become true.

If only you knew!

I am me.

Who are you?

I see myself brown & true.

Who are you?

One of many, who can never be you.

—TATIANA "SUNSHINE" FARROW

27

BLINDED

an eye for an eye
seems we'd all be blind
the sights we seek
but is that what we find?

words of life often mislead
we only understand
when understanding is dead

the anger controls
when soft voices speak
we can't stop to listen
to show you are weak

in public we are who
we try to be most
alone, we are still
who we try not to see

half of what is in our minds
is none of our business
can't we handle our own
or is it we who can't handle this?

now I can't go back
it was my choice to leave
on account of my pride
never could we be

an eye for an eye
seems we've both been blind
the sights we seek
or is this all we'll find?

—REBECCA SULIN

28

LIFE SUCKS

It's been way too long for me to stop
To think about what is going on in me
All I know is . . .

It Sucks
You Suck
We All Suck
Life Sucks

The world is just pocket change for the realtors
Love has become a profit for the so called poets
Happiness has become a bottled product

It Sucks
You Suck
We All Suck
Life Sucks

I'm drowning in all my apathy
I'm diving into the gutters of hell
I try to swim to sanctuary, and still . . .

It Sucks
You Suck
We All Suck
Life Sucks

—BABELICIOUS

Chapter 2
Aaaaaaaaaargh!!!
I Hate You!

UNTITLED

For once I am happy
But this only lasts for a second or two
Now, I feel a burning sensation
This pain is caused by you

You, who I once trusted
I gave you the key to my heart
You opened it many times
But now you broke it apart

You can't keep it from tearing
Just let it fall away,
After it goes, I will have to die
This is it, so I'll say good-bye

I can't stop the tears from falling
It stings and numbs my face
I can't do a thing about it
Someone, please, take me away from this sad and
   lonely place

If you could only love me back
You could learn it's not too late
I still love you, you know
No, I lied and all I feel for you is hate

—L

PAIN IN THE ASS

What have I done to you,
for you to treat me this way?
Is there something I can do?
Something I can say?

In all my life,
as weird as it may be,
I have never met someone
so completely confusing to me.

You make me laugh,
you make me cry,
you get me pissed,
whenever you lie.

You get on my nerves,
like smeared lip gloss,
or food in your teeth,
when you got no floss.

I don't know why I like you;
you're such a pain in the ass.
I'm hoping this is just a crush,
and that it soon will pass.

. . . But I'm way past a crush now.
It's almost been four years.
The love of my life is turning out to be
one of my biggest fears.

—ASHLEY BURKETT

YOUR EFFECT ON ME

When I look at you
When I read your words
From deep inside me
Something rises

When you look at me
When you touch me
From deep inside
Something rises

When you look at my ass
When you let your eyes wander
From deep inside
Something rises

From all the things that make you
To all the things you are
I am sure of one thing,
You make me want to VOMIT!

—CREA

ODE TO A NARCISSIST

mirror, mirror, on the wall
mirror, mirror, in the hall
mirror, mirror, on the ceiling
you haven't lost that lovin' feeling ...
as you stare at your reflection
and profess your deep affection
I wonder if I should tell you
no one loves you quite like you do ...

you have framed pictures on your shelf
they're not of me, they're of yourself
on my birthday, you gave me a sweater
and bought yourself a brand-new Jetta
Christmas presents under the tree
I stupidly thought they might be for me
while deep inside I really knew
you bought them all to give to you
you tell me each and every day
you're beautiful in every way
your golden hair, your perfect lips
your super taste in art
your little one-track heart ...
and with your pretty hazel eyes
I hope one day you realize
(though it may take time for you to see)
THAT YOU ARE NOT AS CUTE AS ME!

—JESSIKAH DRAGON

35

BETTER WITHOUT ME

You're better without me
Go on and live your fake little life
No one else can see who you are, except me
You're better without me

Tell your lies
Ruin innocent people's lives
Tell your stories
There is really nothing more to it
Go on without a care in the world
'Cause one day I know it'll all catch up
  with you
You're better without me

I won't stop you anymore
I won't try to make you see
I will forget you, I will

You're sad when someone leaves you
But did you ever really give a #!&@?
Please pretend you don't care
Please don't shed a tear
You move on like nothing ever happened
I know you're hollow inside
You're better without me

One day when you wake up
And no one is there for you anymore
'Cause they got tired of being treated like &@%$.
Look at yourself
Ask yourself if you like what you see
You'll be alone, and as you taught me
There are no second chances
Think of me then, and
Know I'm better off without you.

—ASHLEY N. LORENZI

ERASE

I wasted precious moments,
spending them with you.
You told me so many lies,
and nothing you said was true.

Eight months I wasted,
now I throw them in the trash.
I wish it was that easy,
and I could erase that past.

Erase that we ever talked,
or that we even met,
that I let you boss me around.
All of it, I regret.

I could have done much better,
but I settled for much less.
We took a wrong turn somewhere,
and now I'm quite a mess.

I don't know why I loved you,
or even gave a #$%*.
You took my love for granted,
and never cared one bit.

Pretty soon we will see each other,
every single day.
When I see you, I won't care,
I'll turn the other way.

When our paths cross,
I won't take a glance.
You've changed into someone else,
and threw away your chance.

Now I lie in bed,
completely wide awake.
It's midnight and all I can do
is think, what a huge mistake.

—ASHLEY BURKETT

STILL A LITTLE BOY

You're still a little boy
Don't let your imagination take you away
Thought you now looked older
But your actions are still the same

You need your friends to back you up
You need a girl that is not so bright
You need Mom and Dad, especially on paycheck night
You even need your big bro, to teach and defend
   with all his might

Those points right there
Prove my point straight
You're not any older
Than you were when you turned eight

You'll wake up one day
On the right side of the bed
You'll know what to do
Not like before, dunno yet

So, my dear boy
Don't take offense
You're not all that
Face the facts, it's not happening yet!

—DRAGANA N. BIJEDIĆ

40

CORY

I see you, but do you see me?
You mean so much
I can't explain
I think about you often
But nothing comes to mind
You say, "I love you."
I'm sure you say that to everyone ...
Jessica, Joanelle, Crystal, Shauna ...
Where does the list end?
You say there's no one else
Liar
"I want to meet you."
Does that sound familiar?
"Are you as gorgeous as I remember?"
That—I want to know!
You don't love me
You need me
I'm there for you
Your house, food, transportation
A good #%@$.
I think about you every day.
I love you.
I hate you!

—JESSICA LAUNDERVILLE

NOW

You have no idea,
Of the $%#* you put me through,
As you watch and laugh,
I sit here alone and miss you.

You actually had me going,
And thinking that you cared.
My heart had just been broken,
With your lies it was repaired.

Then I heard a rumor,
That I had just been used,
My heart was more than broken,
But it was very badly bruised.

Now I see how you are,
And not your little act,
You are such a #%?*$&@ player,
And that, my dear, is a fact.

I feel so abused,
And so very, very dumb.
I wish I could go back to the days,
When you called me "awesome."

—ASHLEY BURKETT

FRIEND OR FOE

Are you my friend, or are you my foe?
Please tell me now, 'cuz I want to know.
One minute you are there, the next you are gone.
I can't take this any longer, this can't go on.

Friends are supposed to be there for you,
This is something I know.
How can you say things behind my back,
Then turn around and act nice?

How come you act phony all the time?
How come I'm the only one who knows you lie?
Why can't you be a good friend?
Forget about being popular, because it doesn't matter
    in the end.

—DANIELLE MARIE VACCA

MY WORST ENEMY

Girl, you think you got me good
but hon, if you only knew
all the things that people say
about what you say, wear and do

I know I am not always right
and I know I'm not the best
but when I look at some of your outfits
at least I know I am better dressed

You talk about me 2 other people
even my friends who will tell
I know everything you utter
Tramp, go to hell!

You try to cut me down
you try to take my man
but honey, he loves ME
you're one of his many fans

I have the urge to hit you
to throw you down the stairs
to punch your teeth down your throat
and pull out all your hairs

But I know you'll get yours
someone else will give you a pound
for I know I am better
and what comes around goes around

—LAUREN K. DANEK

DEAR PAT

I don't wanna see your %$#&*! face
No more
Cuz I'm trying to forget
The %$#* we did before

You made me feel like a Queen
'Til you got what you came for
I hope you're #%?*$&@ happy
Now I feel like a #%?*$&@ whore

You stupid goddamn bastard
I hate your #%?*$&@ guts
You stay the hell away from me
Or I'll cut off your
#%?*$&@ nuts

You used me up, and threw me out
Something I thought you'd never do
Now I see that's just a part
Of you being you

I hate you so, so much
But I still like you too
If someone had to be so mean to me
Why the hell did it have to be you?

—ASHLEY BURKETT

WHY WOULD HE WANT YOU?

I want to scratch your eyes out with my fingernails,
Or to make you wish you were dead, if killing you fails.
You *!#$%^^# back-stabbing bitch!
I want to kill you and throw you in a ditch!
You ripped my heart out,
Then threw it on the ground.
I want to scream and scream, but I don't make a sound.
You knew how I felt about that guy.
Now that you hurt me so bad, I want you to die!
What compels you to do the things you do?
He has me now, why the hell would he want you?
Back off you ugly whore,
Because one of these days,
You'll have your heart slammed in a door!

—AMANDA KAY ROBERTSON

46

THE WEDDING GIFT

Like a pill, I can't stomach you—
the Green Monster
stabs me with jealousy
and serves my heart
on a platter.

Like a serpent,
I rise
from Eden's garden
and proclaim,
"I am life! I am all!"
I hiss at this and
see the endless blue sky,
which I swim to.

Propelled forward in time,
I see your chastity ruined
by this bitch, which calls
herself woman.

I am woman,
my tongue wishes to taste you.
Be tempted by me.
Give into seduction.

The whore who holds your heart
will die a worm on a hook,
as I cast her into the sea
to her imminent death.

You foul slut, I'm through!
There will be no wedding bells today!

—HEATHER E. NYHOF

I JUST TURN AWAY

I don't pay attention,
I let her say what she wants to say,
because he's on my side,
& I just turn away.

I never did anything to her,
we were friends before.
Now she's a dumb bitch,
that stupid, nasty whore.

She said some mean things,
but I let her say what she wants to say.
I stick my nose in the air,
& I just turn away.

That stupid, fat bitch,
can take all of her lies,
shove them up her ass,
along with her apple pies.

I never say one thing,
I let her say what she wants to say.
Then rub on him to piss her off,
& I just turn away.

I'd love to punch her in the face,
but I won't stoop that low . . .
but it would feel sooo good,
to hit that stupid ho.

But I act mature,
let her say what she wants to say,
keep a smile on my face,
& I just turn away.

She makes my days a living hell,
with all her childish games.
She thinks she's gonna hurt me,
with those stupid little names.

One of these days she'll need me,
and I'll say what I want to say,
"Go #$@* yourself, you stupid bitch!"
& I'll just turn away.

—ASHLEY BURKETT

CHAPTER 3

LOVE AND
DEEP THOUGHTS

ONE THOUGHT TO HELP

Outside the wind swirls
Soft leaves do tumble
Watch as you walk
Beware of where you stumble

Know now are good times
Listen to birds sing
Love friends and family
Enjoy the small things

Stay clear of the dark road
Believe in all hope
Keep focused and clear
This isn't a joke

Take a long walk
See nature's colors
Live for life
And love one another

—THERESA J. VANDERMEER

THE SWEET AGE

A period of sunshine
Without a trace of rain
What's often seen as joyous
Contains amounts of pain

Often called the sweet age
Can often seem so sour
Leaving a bitter taste
That hurts to devour

An age without logic and reason
Struggling to find your place
Trying to fit in the puzzle
Of the body's urging race

Waiting to conquer the sweet age
To leave its anguish behind
To journey into easier times
With a lighter peace of mind.

—GLENESSA TAYLOR

IN THE PAST

Forget his name, forget his past
Forget his kiss and warm embrace
Forget his love that you once knew
Remember now, there is someone new
Forget the love you once shared
Forget the fact he once cared
Forget the time you spent together
Remember now, he is gone forever
Forget how you cried all night long
Forget how close you once were
Remember now, he's close to her
Forget the way he used to walk
Forget the way he used to talk
Forget the way he spoke your name
Remember now, he is not the same
Forget he used to hold your hand
Forget the sweetness, if you can
Forget the times that went so fast
Remember now, he is in the past!

—CORTNEY A. CALIGUR

ME

Every feeling, every emotion . . .
I have red hair. I have my father's eyes, my mother's
hands. I have crooked teeth, and blue eyes. I like to
draw. I like the color of wine. I've cheated, but my
hair is still red, and my teeth are still crooked, and
I probably won't always like the color of wine.

I have strong muscles. I have lips that always smile. I
have veins that bleed. I babble when I am nervous. I
feel other people's pain, but I cry for no reason. I
like open flames. I've been stubborn since I was a
child. I'm from Montana, but I hate the cold. I've
cheated on diets. I've lied, but I bleed and my lips
still smile, and my muscles won't always be so strong.

I have a chubby face. I have fair skin. I have a
German face that I borrowed from my grandmother. I
have long nails that break regularly. My feet are
strange. I write. I used to make wreaths from
dandelions. I brush my hair too much. I have cheated
on tests. I fake flirtatious French accents, but I still
have pale skin and my nails break, and I probably
won't always have a chubby face, and I may not always
write, but maybe I will start making wreaths from
dandelions again.

—KRISTA MARIE ROLL

I HAVE TO BE ME

I don't like football
or televised sports
I don't like running
or basketball courts

I do like the rain
and watching it fall
I do like writing
and taking calls

I don't have to like football
or televised sports
I don't have to like running
or basketball courts

I don't have to be you
I have to be me
I am all I've got left
Who else can I be?

—RACHEL DANIELLO

IF

If I were love
If I were joy
If I were all the happy things
If I were peace
If I were harmony
If I were the product of imagination
If . . .
I'd clone myself!

—MARISSA BERLIN

FIRST LOVE

This was my first
I hope not my last
He snuck through my dreams
And changed my past

I felt like I knew him
From a childhood thought
He was given from God
Not just a toy that was bought

I looked into his eyes
As he looked into mine
I had stumbled into love
For the very first time

I took him to dinner
His meal was quite lumpy
But of course, it would be
He was my first puppy!

—BETHANY SULLENS

FEET

Feet come in every shape and size
Some could even win the Nobel prize
Some feet are so interesting
They have to be memorized
Some feet are so scary
They make you terrified
Some feet can harmonize
Some feet can sing lullabies
But my feet ... my feet are idolized

—ALISON DENNO

59

CREED

Walking up slowly
Steps that are untraced
Betrayed

Footprints
To altars
Where fake gods
Play joker

Christ

Who carries books
And prayers
But failing to deliver

A name
Without surrealism
Means nothing to a wanderer

—JESSICA M. TISRON

NOTHING

Split my heart open wide
And feed it to the nerves of God
So I can feel

Kneeling in a dark abode
of my mind
I dig myself deeper
Still, I cannot feel

I am demented, and twisted
Split me inside
If I could just say one thing,
It would be that I have nothing to hide.

—TABI, TRIBAL WARRIOR

STREAMED "ODE" CONSCIOUSNESS

I'm getting on my yak machine
Because the pre-adolescent apes are hounding me
I feel blue
Because I hate you
    and all the others

It makes me smile
    all the while
      I'm urinating on the ceiling
Sewing a quilt of my teenage angst

stitch, stitch, stitch, DEATH

and throwing away the cow, hey some hay!

Moo, moo, moo CHOMP!

A cow symbolizes my love for the world, soon to be destroyed and consumed

I say, the hay, is a symbol of the day, in which I sit
     by the bay,

thinking of how I just make, make things out of
CLAY!

. . . Damn, claymation is cool.

Like that show on MTV with the cave people. I like T-Rex.

I am a trash can with no arms, two legs, eating a
     purple Jehovah's witness.

What am I?

—JET DENNIE

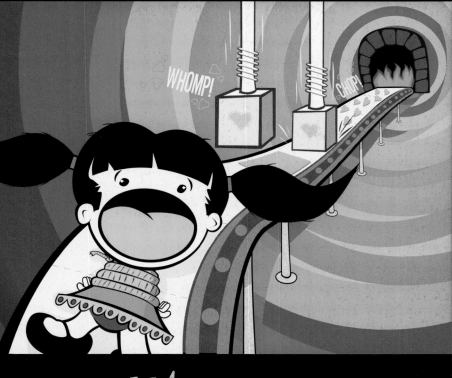

CHAPTER 4
CRUSHED

BUS #819 HOLLAND AMERICA LINE

It's raining in Alaska
and the motor homes drive past
on never-ending crusades
across this highway
of trees so thick
they crowd each other out
for want of sunlight,
and few have branches
save for the very top.

The air here is clean,
but I can barely breathe.
Every exhalation is followed
by "Let it go, Amber."
I've been shaky lately,
and yesterday, when he walked by,
I started quivering
as though scared for my life.
It would come over me in waves
and no amount of clothing or blankets
could relieve me of it.

I feel sick,
and I can't eat.
My stomach turns at the thought of food.
What has he done to me,
and in just one week ...
just one night?

And how do I convince myself
that e-mail will suffice?
Every time I play the scene
out in my head,
it gets better
and soon, I will have forgotten
what really happened.

The rain has filled the edges
of this lonely highway
we are traveling with our own zip code.
Every time we pass through a town,
we double its population.

Things here whisper his name,
like the windshield wipers and birds;
everything reminds me of him.
So many inescapable coincidences.
The next four days loom ahead
as though a prison sentence—
my jail, the most beautiful place on earth.

It's like I've fallen into a pit
and he is darkness.
Concentration on anything else is a joke.
At this second,
I want nothing more in the whole world,
and I'm wishing like hell
that I hadn't given up
on the idea of God.

—AMBER NICOLE LUPIN

I WANT

I want you like a lemonade
wants another sour lemon
I want you like a drinker wants
another glass of gin
I want you like an astronaut
wants to set foot on the moon
I want you like an addict wants
another shot of sin.

When you look at me, I can't look back
I turn away and grin
When you touch me, I can't touch back
but you know I really want to

You're a daisy chain
behind a windowpane
I'm like a spoiled child, always wanting more
don't close the door
I wanna walk with you across the beach
I wanna hold your hand, but I can't quite reach

—REBECCA FURNELL

NO MORE

U took my head
U took my heart
Since you've left
I've fallen apart

I don't go anywhere
Or do anything
I sit by the phone
And hope it'll ring

After I gave up
About a month without u
U decided to call me
Just out of the blue

And in that call
U decided to say
U really missed me
But u were moving away

When the call was over
And we said our good-byes
A million tears
Fell from my eyes

I hung up the phone
And fell to the ground
Because no more
Would u be around

No more u to hug me
Or give me a kiss
But I will always remember u
And u, I will eternally miss.

—ASHLEY BURKETT

AWW

Aww is never enough
Aww means that you really don't care
Complain about your own problems, and disregard mine
They mean nothing to you
Aww is not sincere
Not a cure
Or little noise of happiness
Or sympathy
It's something to fill the void
Of feeling . . .
Anything
Three aww's are not enough
I'm spilling my heart out to you
There you are
Blankly staring, without expression
Aww

—ANGELINE VUONG

70

CHEM 101
(LABORATORY LOVE)

The acid in my beaker is dilute
The boy who sits in front of me is cute
He doesn't notice my flirtatious winks
'Cause he's focusing on phosphorus and zinc
He says the charge of calcium is two
I tell him, "I have chemistry with you!"
He doesn't understand the way I feel
(He thinks the nuclei have sex appeal)
But I think about him every day in class
When he is looking up atomic mass
And when he states the formula for density
I want him with a passionate intensity
I've never met a boy who is as smart
but he's got a TI-90 for a heart
Of him I am becoming rather fond
I wish that we could form a double bond
But the boy does not reciprocate my crush
He is busy cleaning test tubes with a brush
Still my faith remains in one small fact . . .
One day, he'll find out that opposites do attract.

—JESSIKAH DRAGON

WHAT DO I HAVE TO DO?

What do I have to do
To make you see
That you are the perfect guy for me?
I'll do whatever it takes
Just to have your love
I'm not asking for a couple of years
Because things aren't going to get better

If I could only fast-forward our lives
Would we still be together?
I'm willing to take that chance
Just to have a chance with you
Some things I want to give up
Thinking I'll never have you
But I'm not a quitter
I just have to make you see
You're the perfect guy for me
I'll wait as long as I need
I don't know what else to do
To prove how much I love you
So, I'll ask you one more time
What do I have to do?

—ERICA MORGAN

SUBMERGED IN TEARS

My heart grows weary
Thinking of you
And making a theory

My heart, being weary
So has my life, it's so dreary
For my heart's own desire
It wants nothing more
Just security, sincerity, sanctuary

I admire the way it used to be
Having you there, here with me
I had you to myself
Before the world came and took you
Leaving me in agony

Missing you has now become my hobby
It's what I do best
It's part of my life
Even in rest,
I am submerged in tears.

—BRITTNEY PALMER

73

JUST DREAMING

Last night I dreamt
of you and me.
We went to Hawaii
and swam in the sea.

We went to the movies,
and you held my hand.
We drove down a winding road,
in the country land.

You made me dinner.
You were such a great cook.
You told me you loved me,
Like it was straight from a book.

Last night I dreamt
That you were mine.
As long as we were together,
everything was fine.

We went to Magic Mountain,
and went on all the rides.
I told you my secrets,
'cause in you I could confide.

I woke up this morning,
not quite the same,
'cause I came to realize
you don't even know my name.

—JULIE GOODMAN

UNTITLED

You are the one who knew my biggest fears
You were the reason I shed all those tears
Every night, as I cry
I'm hoping I will die
I am so close to death
When will I breathe my last breath?
Can't you see my blank expression
I've fallen deep into depression
I still love you
My love for you will always be true
I love you so much
I no longer can feel your touch
When I had your love
I felt like an angel from above
But all those things are yours, and no longer mine
I knew it would only take time
Love is such a crime!

—LAUREN

75

WHY?

Since you left me, all I do is cry
Why did you leave, why oh why?

I gave you my all,
And in return, I received one call

A call that destroyed our love,
Our love no longer flew like a dove

It crashed, dived into the ground
So fast, without warning or a sound

One minute we were floating,
The next minute I sunk, and he was gloating

Oh, why did you leave me, say it isn't so
Without your love, I am feeling really low

Please come back, and relieve me from this pain
I am a desert, and you are the rain.

—BECKY PEYTON

UNTITLED

I want you, but I don't want you to just want me the way I want you. I want you to want me the way you want me, do you want that? And I don't want you to want me because I want you, but because you want me and need me. I need you, and I want you to want it in the way I want, and don't say I can't want to want you, because I want you, whether or not you want it, because I know you need me to want you, and I know you need to want the way I need to want you, and I always get what I want, because I need to want.

—IZZY

OVER

I saw you staring
at me across the room.
You just dumped me,
what should I assume?

Guess what, Babe?
I am over you!
As far as I'm concerned,
me and you are through.

For today and tomorrow,
this week and next year,
'cuz falling in love with you again
is my biggest fear.

So, do me a favor,
and stay away from me.
I don't want to be hurt again.
So, please let me be.

I'm not trying to be mean,
I just don't wanna cry,
'cuz I get a sting in my heart,
every time you walk by.

I remember,
as you stood there,
staring at the ground.
I was excited inside,
but I did not make a sound.

I remember the time;
I remember the place;
I remember my feeling inside;
when that look spread upon your face.

You looked so good,
in your T-shirt and jeans.
I remember that night,
you were in my dreams.

I wish I could be with you;
every nite and day,
because I love you,
more than words can say.

When I looked into your eyes,
I knew it was true,
my heart never lies,
I was in love with you.

—ASHLEY BURKETT

79

SEASONS' CRIME

My hands leave my side
and reach for yours
only to find myself
grabbing the past
Painful
   Rough
      Emotional.

Where is the soft, smooth, gentle skin
that my hands long to touch?

The hands that gloved mine
during the chilling
windy circulations
of snow and wind, of Wintertime

The hands I clutched for guidance,
while avoiding walking through
Spring's muddy puddles.

The hands that brought me the seashells
with sincerity,
found beside the summer's blue beaches.

The hands that helped gather leaves
with no hesitation,
as Autumn came to an end,

Those fingers that wiped away
my tears
and sadness altogether,

With arms that took away
the pain
and strife.

By the mind that taught me about
love, hate
and life.

The heart that let me feel
all the emotions
in the world

But those hands ...

The hands that stole my heart
leaving fingerprints
all over
my life.

—RAISSA MAE SAGUN

81

CHAPTER 5
WHY ME?!

MY YOUTH

My youth
had a mind of its own.
Consisted of summers
that were like springs
and springs that
were like winters,
and the winters
went by so fast,
and ice was my friend.

There were lazy days
filled with Cadillac Sin,
and golden sun-sprayed mornings,
cold, embalmed nights.
There were days with
only twenty-three hours,
deep, milky twilights
and ravenous sunrises.

Sometimes I woke up
wondering where I was,
and sometimes
my eyelids were taped shut,
but I was always looking.
I was always searching
for something my
adolescent mind
couldn't half comprehend.

We were all rushing,
striving to be members
of that elite adulthood.
We couldn't know,
or be told.

And how many times
did they tell us?
I had cotton in my ears,
but I was always listening.
I guess I'll never know.

I was so fragile,
but I never drew back
the curtains.
My bones wept
for eyes that remained dry.
I was so thick and full,
but no one knew.
Every day was a lie.
One big teenage lie.

—AMBER NICOLE LUPIN

BLAH

I want to kill myself
But for some reason I can't
I hate feeling this way
'Cause all I do is rant

It's stupid; it's dumb
Why must I always feel this way?
I can't feel now, I'm numb
And it starts over every day

Whenever it's gone
It comes back to bite me in the ass
Whenever I feel happy
It comes back really fast

It's stupid; it's dumb
Why must I feel this way?
I can't feel now, I'm numb
And it starts over every day

It's like a phase,
I'm happy, then I am sad.
It keeps on going in a circle,
But it always ends up bad.

—JULIE GOODMAN

MATURITY SICKNESS

Testing myself,
pushing the limits.
How much farther can I go?
Today's a good day,
but tomorrow won't be so ...
wonderful.
I failed again.
It's because of radiation;
too much exposure can kill you.
I'm too young,
this small body
has no idea what to do.
Is this worth it?
Are you?
I never thought I'd be where I am today.
What happened
to story time and play?
Step up, and face the monster,
this world.
Kindergarten was so much fun,
wouldn't it be nice to go back?
The times we had, that were carefree,
lacking pressure;
the ticking nuisance of expectations.
Youth awaiting suicide.
Assessing life and its worth.
Oh, how meaningless.

—ANGELINE VUONG

TUESDAY AFTERNOON

Your fuzzy dice twirl
as we pass G and 18th.
The lights of all time
are burning in your eyes
and I can't even hear
the utterance from
that hollow place in your car.
8
Just like that laminated copy
of Van Gogh's "Starry Night"
on my ceiling.
So old.
2
We creep past places we've been,
in times of happiness.
Hard gravel under firm tires
and doleful stares
out of vitrified windows.
7
My hands fly to my ears,
and my throat is screaming no,
over and over again;
a fierce epileptic fit of will,

drowning out your radio,
your words, your air conditioning.
And people are staring.
Staring like they'd never seen
someone dying.
4
My cheek tingles and then
fills with hot blood.
My chin is wet, but my eyes
have gone dry.
Yellow light and screeching.
You are talking again.
6
And then my feet,
feet to the ground,
grass and pavement,
and the sun on my back.
My mind clear and I do nothing,
but look straight ahead.
0

—AMBER NICOLE LUPIN

SUBURBAN SUICIDE

When one saga ends, new ones begin
A circle of confusion, I can never win
Hate is the root of all that is me
I will never know why this must be
I long for death to take me away
The black night captures the day
From love to hate, and good to bad
As the seasons change, I become sad
With one shot to the head
So long, and I am dead.

—AJA WATSON

IF TEARS WEREN'T CLEAR

If tears weren't clear
She'd have to wear a mask
Her face would be stained
The way they stain glass
She'd be dis-
Colored and ugly
Then they can all see . . .
How sick and pathetic is she
Yet, she is really me

—KAREN GATHANY

NOT MY DAY

My cereal was soggy.
My eggs were cold.
The juice was sour.
The bread was old.
I was late 4 homeroom,
Rushing down the hall
The heel of my shoe broke,
And I took a fall.
The rain fell hard
On me and my clothes.
It ruined my hair
And gave me a runny nose.
I failed a test
On the history of France.
I got caught on a nail
And ripped my pants.
I went home early.
I couldn't take it anymore.
I was cold and wet,
And my pants were torn.
I went to bed and began to pray,
Please make tomorrow a much better day.

—CORTNEY A. CALIGUR

ALL BY MYSELF

My friend is gone, she says I'm not what she needs
I am confused and lost, like one floating leaf
Why must I change the person I am inside?
I am a body, in which a lost soul sadly presides

I may be quiet and shy, but does that make me a snob?
I may not be small, but does that make me a fat blob?
Why must happiness depend on what they say is so?
They push me in to a dark room, in which my shine can't glow

Why must our friendship revolve around your disposition's choice?
I may not be much, but I am a person who feels and has a voice
I will always be there, when your problems leave you lost and alone
But for now, I am a soul with an empty prairie to wander and roam

What they say should not decide who we are to be
We are people, but with your eyes you do not clearly see
The more friends the happier you are, but are they real?
Or are you a phase that will disappear with only a wound to heal?

Go away! I will not! I am a person and my voice they will hear
I am not what they say, and am only filled with a fear
I am not a shadow, but an individual who knows what is true
But I am hurt by the loss of us, and the growth of just you

—APES

UGLY

Scratch
Scratch
Scratch
all this work for nothing
I turn on the music
so I don't
have to hear my thoughts
(belittling)
wash; I feel naked
but at least I am clean
shedding my skin
not my problems
three months of hard work
hours in front of the mirror
all for nothing
I am so disappointed
I can't even see my own ribs!
I hate this feeling
Bashing
(myself)
Belittling
(everyone is)
But in a way I worship it
I think
Maybe

If I get up off my
(fat ass, fat ass, fat ass)
It will finally motivate me
(ugly, ugly, ugly)
this feeling (not myself, or someone like me)
this feeling
wash with hot water, so hot that it burns
but at least I feel alive
and not dead
I've lost, but I've gained
I'm dying, yet I am living
will (I don't have one)
I ever stop feeling this way?
all this work for nothing
all I feel is my skin
and flesh
hanging off my bones
and the hot (not me)
shower water scalding my skin
as I try to wash myself away
myself
this feeling
empty, yet filling
hating, but craving.

—DAITVIA HOLBRIONA

UNTITLED

Today, she felt like a woman; he made her.
Yesterday, she felt like a child; she made her.
Tomorrow, she doesn't know.

All these irrelevant feelings roaming inside her ...
Searching for a place to meet.
She separates herself to find she is neither
        woman nor child ...
        neither yolk nor egg ...
        but definitely in a delicate shell.

Today, the woman just wanted someone to #%$*.
Yesterday, the child just wanted to play.
Tomorrow, she'll try both.
(She doesn't know the difference.
Neither of them care.)

Sometimes neither of them feel,
But often, both feel simultaneously
And it scrambles her,
Scrambles her mind
Confuses her body ... the small-hipped,
        flat-chested thing
with only one burning hole to escape through.

—SUGARSTAR

UNTITLED

Case Study #1

Perverted man in the corner. He smirks. It's all the same: another day sitting, looking, and thinking. He thinks so much, he's thought himself right into a straight line. He smiles into blankness with his thoughts. It's all the same to him, even in an art museum with timeless and worthless art engulfing him. It's all the same to him, nothing changes. Not the art, not the people who come to see it, and certainly not himself.

Case Study #2

A young boy, about the age of eighteen. He's perplexed and pondering the meaning of life. His newspaper stares at him while he turns to look at the book the man next to him is reading. It may be an excuse to look at something else. No one really knows what's going on in the head of someone staring, not the victim, not the other people staring around them, and certainly not himself.

(continued)

(continued)

Case Study #3

A woman lying near the exterior of her house. She's about fifty-three, trying to be twenty. The facade definitely does not suit her. Her liver spots look designed on her skin, as if it were meant to be a mosaic. The sun could only add to the wonderful masterpiece on her hands. She bops her head untimely to Art Blakey. Her sex appeal died years ago, but it is okay, since the sun doesn't notice, nor the rhythms, and certainly not herself.

Case Study #4

Uncertain, insecure young woman. She hides in the corner, scribbling her inhibitions and secrets. She's quite impressionable, and not at all. She lives a schizophrenic life, and gets away with it as just being moodiness or flightiness. Sometimes her life is split directly down the middle, between lies and truth. Sometimes it's all the same difference. In reality, no one knows when to really listen, not the strangers, not the people who know her, not the people who want to know her, and certainly not myself.

— QUEEN B

THIS MORNING

there is a ring
around the sun today
and the air is permeated
with the stench of an herb
half the kids here
have checked to make sure it's not them

my eyes are down today
low and out of the way

out from the stares of people
I have stopped caring for
because they don't care
about me

I keep my face heavy
in the hope that someone
will look my way
and grant me solace
I will not ask in words
I will not show my weakness
I can be sad and strong
I must

I keep this look of hurt on my face
because it is easier
easier to leave it there, than take it off
easier to be crushed, and look crushed
easier to pretend you're not ...
I want someone to be there for me
and deny those in the attempt

(continued)

(continued)

I inhale deeply
desperately trying to take in
the air's quality this morning
to take the edge off my thoughts
to take the hurt from
my mind
my head

I don't pay attention to myself
to writing assignments I will not do
tests I will not pass
the truth is my apathy
has made life unbearable
the hard, wooden desk is
jamming into my ribs as I lie
bent over on it
frantically scribbling
meaningless thoughts on dirty paper

I think about changing
myself and my life
I think about
not going to class
I think about taking lots of drugs
I think about sleeping in
for the rest of time
I think about not waking up
and enjoying the silence

I wish the sun's orb would consume me
this morning
swallow me up and take me
to the stars and beyond
I would hold on
to the ring of light
to wherever it takes me

I look up and smile
a smile not for the people
that brush past me in the halls
but for the thought that maybe that circle
could, would take me into the sky

I stare at it longingly
and think how I would disappear
without regret
just fade into the sky
never to be seen again
I shut my eyes, and turn away
sharply aware of the absurdity
I bow my head, and sink
off, to go live the rest of my life.

—AMBER NICOLE LUPIN

ANGST!

In ancient Greek times, poets were considered the mortal beings clos— to the gods. Today, th—

PlanetKiki.com. Banding— from various corners of th— they remind us of the powe— —dom, and peace to be fu—

CHAPTER 6

POETRY 101

Do you have overwhelming feelings that frustrate you beyond belief? Feel as if you might burst if you don't get them out of you? Feel the need to change the world, and everyone involved? Does everything around you inspire strong opinions? Or are you so confused sometimes that you just feel blank? If you have said yes to any one of these questions, move ahead and become the master of your destiny; indulge in the art of poetry!

CAN I BE A POET?

Yes, you can! Within all of us a poet resides; whether we take notice is a matter of choice. A poet is anyone who chooses to express her or his appreciation and understanding of all the wonders of life, and of the beyond—anything that can be felt, thought, or dreamed. Living to feel every moment deeply and intensely, a poet devours all the beauty that life has to offer. She or he understands that within that beauty is a spectrum of emotions, ideas, and possibilities that can evoke everything from the most profound agonies to the most transcending epiphanies.

To be a poet you only need a yearning to understand the world around you. After all, poetry is the music of the soul, which everyone is capable of tuning in to;

BACK IN THE DAY, IT WAS POPULAR FOR POETS TO USE SKULLS AS INSPIRATIONAL DECOR

words are merely one way to express oneself.

Although the craft of poetry and its clichés insinuate that you must be a deeply sensitive and anguished soul armed with a pen, the passion of a poet can come through in many forms: music, dance, sculpture, film, painting, or zoology; it is anything that inspires one to create a message from one's soul. On the less dramatic side, a poet is anyone who accepts and expresses that life is funny, sad, absurd, aggravating, sexy, happy, boring, and powerful.

If this all sounds good to you so far, and being a poet is right up your alley, the next step is accepting the challenge of living like a poet. This means thinking and sharing what moves you. Whether it is your agonies, joys, experiences, philosophies, or anything else, take a moment to think about what you want to share with the world. Then, explain why and how those things compel you.

_____

_____

_____

_____

_____

_____

_____

_____

_____

OKAY, I'M A POET. NOW WHAT?

Now that you've got your motivation, it's time to open your eyes and start to see the world as one big poetic time bomb waiting to explode. Yes, sugar, it's time to crack yourself open, heart and mind, and find poetry streaming in and out and throughout your life. Living life as a poet is all a matter of attitude and perspective. So say okay, and greet your muse today!

THREE GREEK MUSES OF POETRY:

CALLIOPE – EPIC POETRY

EUTERPE – LYRIC POETRY

EROS – LOVE POETRY

A muse is a Greek goddess believed to inspire artistic genius. There were nine muses in total, and three specifically assigned to poetry.

NATURE

Among the most obvious places to look for inspiration is nature. From the wondrous world around you to the mysterious microcosms within, interacting with and observing the world can be keys to unlocking emotions. Whether you choose to spend an afternoon lying about to take in the purity of the autumn air, ride your bike in a rainstorm, or absorb the desolate beauty of haunted forests; surrounding yourself in nature's energy is a surefire way to invigorate yourself with the power of life.

Name three things you love in nature and say why they move you:

1.

2.

3.

SITUATIONS

Summoning your muse sometimes requires taking matters into your own hands and using the pain, ennui, joy, and depth of what you go through in your day-to-day life as inspiration. After all, experiences are what make you grow, and learning from every moment is a phenomenon to savor! Listen to your favorite songs on repeat, and purge yourself of duress; dive into the past with old photo albums, even if they aren't yours (nothing beats nostalgia, even if the memories are borrowed); submerge yourself in the mystique of travel; or dwell on the details of daily despair. Call the muse to you by practicing what you love.

List three of your most inspiring activities and what they bring to you:

1.

2.

3.

BEINGS

Whether it is your best friend, that special someone, historical figures, family, strangers, or your absolutely pulchritudinous kitty who brings you to a new level of understanding, inspiration from others is always available. Because every individual contains an infinity within her- or himself, learning can be a never-ending social adventure! Bond with friends over late-night French fries, search for cultural commentary, or just imagine you are someone else—the ideas can keep coming.

Name three beings who inspire you, and why:

1.

2.

3.

OBSERVATIONS

How you see the world matters. After all, perspective is what makes us different from one another, and it is completely unique to you. Gather your observations of what you see, feel, touch, smell, or hear, then use these components to create poems that provoke laughter, tears, or thought. Just ponder the ways of the world, and find your magic waiting. Springboards for commentary include: random headlines of the newspaper, traditions, yourself as you grow, or the funky hairdo formations of diner waitresses.

Identify three observations of yours, and your revelations about them:

1.

2.

3.

THE BEYOND

Who knows what might lie outside of planet Earth, or even what secrets lie within this world? The "beyond" is an infinite resource for theories, opinions, and emotions. Zoning out and exploring those possibilities can always bring you back with lots to say. Imagine yourself with supernatural powers; uncover other dimensions; or just trust that life is a gift. Wherever the realm of your imagination can go, just go!

What are your top three theories about the beyond?

1.

2.

3.

THE REGULARS

Several things in life are inevitable besides taxes and death. Heartbreak, anger, and battling demons are just some examples of the inescapable human experiences that cause a downpour of emotions. On the flip side, there is a slew of splendors that can also provoke the muse, such as the arts, dreams, or love. Throughout history, poets have grasped for words to recreate these experiences. Today, the challenge continues. We are all filled with a lust for life; uncovering and divulging those passions is what poetry is about.

Name three of your top struggles or loves, and express the power they have:

1.

2.

3.

SPIN ON YOUR HEAD UNTIL YOU GET DIZZY.
REPORT YOUR OBSERVATIONS.

As the saying goes, the pen is mightier than the sword. So when it comes to making your weapon work for you, know that there are many styles and methods to choose from, and many ways to express yourself. To help you win your battle for perfectly poignant poems, here are some classic techniques and forms.

TOOLS

Alliteration— A popular poetic method with a tongue-twisting quality. Alliteration is created by stringing together words that begin with the same consonant. Famous poems such as "Beowulf" and Edgar Allan Poe's "The Bells" use alliteration to create a melodious tone. It is also an effective method used throughout "Modern Woman" by Hannah Richards of *ANGST!* (page 6).

DO-IT-YOURSELF ALLITERATION:

Radiation radiates _____ into my _____ ,
(r word, noun)   (r word, noun)

Wrecking the _____ balance of _____ .
(r word, adjective)   (r word, noun)

Assonance— The cousin of alliteration, assonance is created when a poet joins consecutive words in a phrase or line that have similar-sounding vowels. Classic examples of assonance can be found in Lord Tennyson's "The Lotus Eaters" and Shakespeare's "Sonnet LXI." The lines "shove them up her ass,/along with her apple pies" by *ANGST!'s* Ashley Burkett (page 48) is also another sampling of assonance in action.

Couplets— A pair of consecutive lines of rhyming poetry. This common structure can be seen in Geoffrey Chaucer's *Canterbury Tales*, as well as in *ANGST!*'s "Chem 101 (Laboratory Love)" by jessiKah dragon (page 71) and "Why?" by Becky Peyton (page 76).

Dissonance— A collection of unpleasant-sounding words or rhythms. This technique is often used to describe an unpleasant subject. The poem "Ugly" (page 94), by Daitvia Holbriona of *ANGST!*, embodies this method.

Metaphor— A device by which a poet describes one occurrence or object to symbolize another. The thing is, the poet doesn't come right out and say what the symbol stands for; rather the reader must make his or her own conclusion and read into the symbolism to understand what the poet is saying. A prime example of a metaphor is found in *ANGST!* in Raissa Mae Sagun's "Seasons' Crime" (page 80), in which she uses the hands as a symbol of the stages in her broken relationship.

Meter— The pattern or rhythm of a poem. One beat or unit of a meter is known as a foot. The most common poetic meters are:
1. **Iamb:** A two-part beat made of one unstressed syllable followed by one stressed long syllable. Example: you SUCK
2. **Trochee:** A two-part beat with one stressed syllable followed by an unstressed syllable. Example: GIVE me
3. **Dactyl:** A three-part beat made up of one accented syllable followed by two unaccented syllables. Example: GO a-way!
4. **Anapest:** A three-part beat consisting of two unaccented syllables followed by one accented syllable. Example: break-ing DOWN
5. **Spondee:** A two-part beat made up of two accented syllables. Example: SHUT UP

Onomatopoeia— A technique in which a poet uses a word whose sound conveys its meaning—such as *buzz* or *yawn*. For a clear understanding of this device, check out *ANGST!* poet Jet Dennie's "Streamed 'Ode' Consciousness" (page 62).

DO-IT-YOURSELF ONOMATOPOEIA:

Yuck, Yuck, Yuck _____ sucks.
(noun)

I wish I could _____ it with a thousand trucks.
(verb)

It drives me _____ and digs in me deep.
(adjective)

Argh, argh, argh, all I want to do is weep!

Oxymoron— A pair of descriptive words that seem to contradict each other—such as "jumbo shrimp" or Shakespeare's "O heavy lightness."

Parallelism— A device in which the same structure or phrasing repeats line after line. "In the Past" by *ANGST!*'s Cortney A. Caligur (page 54) is an example of this method.

Personification— When a poet gives human qualities to objects, ideas, or animals. Famous poems employing this method are John Milton's *Paradise Lost* and John Keats' "To Autumn."

Sibilance— A kind of alliteration in which hissing sounds are repeated to invoke a particular mood. Soothing the reader with "One Thought to Help" (page 52), poet Theresa J. VanderMeer of *ANGST!* uses sibilance to effectively get her message across.

Simile— Like a metaphor, a simile is a comparison. Instead of implying a comparison symbolically as a metaphor does, a simile is stated in a more straightforward way and includes the word *like* or *as.* "O, My luve's like a red, red rose" is a simile from Robert Burns; *ANGST!*'s Libby Gunter uses a simile in the line "My life is like their dirty water" from her poem "Little Orange Friends" (page 10).

DO-IT-YOURSELF SIMILE:

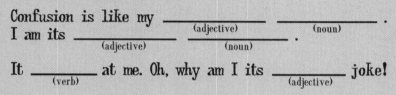

Confusion is like my _____ _____ .
                               (adjective)   (noun)
I am its _____ _____ .
         (adjective)   (noun)

It _____ at me. Oh, why am I its _____ joke!
   (verb)   (adjective)

Stanzas— Just as an essay has paragraphs, some poems have stanzas. Although stanzas are not required, they can help organize narration in longer poems. Check out Amber Nicole Lupin's *ANGST!* poems—"The Whinings of a Lower-Middle Class White Girl" (page 8), "Bus #819 Holland America Line" (page 66), "Tuesday Afternoon" (page 88), "My Youth" (page 84), and "This Morning" (page 99)—to see how the stanzas build momentum with pauses between thoughts and scenarios.

POETIC FORMS

Acrostic— Derived from the Greek words *acros* (topmost) and *stichos* (line of poetry), an acrostic is a play on a word. The Poet chooses one word to create a theme for the poem, then places that word vertically on the page. Each letter of the word then begins a line of horizontal poetry that ties into the theme. Edgar Allan Poe utilizes the acrostic method in his famed poems "Elizabeth" and "A Valentine" by using the names of special ladies in his life to create the pieces.

DO-IT-YOURSELF ACROSTIC:

Annihilate _____,
(noun)

Never to witness their dumb _____.
(noun)

Gone forever is their rancid _____
(noun)

Sending _____ waves of _____ to everyone.
(adjective)   (noun)

Total happiness all over the _____
(noun)

Ballad— Ballads originated as narrative folk poems that retold exciting or romantic tales. They described fatal relationships, supernatural occurrences, and/or outrageous feats of strength. Ballads are still popular today, but they are often set to music; think of Top 40 love songs, and you'll get the gist.

Calligrams— Calligrams are pretty-looking poems that are meant to be viewed. Letters are used like pieces of a collage, with different FONTS and s p a c i n g, and the poems form an image that usually maintains a theme. The French poet Guillaume Apollinaire popularized the form with his complete collection of poems entitled *Calligrammes*, while Allen Ginsberg experimented with calligrams in his poem "Funny Death."

SUGGESTED BALLAD ACCOMPANIMENTS:

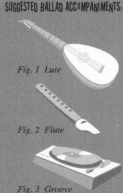

Fig. 1 Lute

Fig. 2 Flute

Fig. 3 Groove

Chant—

A chant is a verse or phrase that is repeated to bring power to the words. It is one of the earliest forms of poetry, used by people throughout the ages as incantations to protect themselves or to gain good luck. The rhythm of a

A BULLHORN CAN MAKE ANY CHANT POEM EXTRA-INSPIRING. TRY YOURS OUT ON THE NEIGHBORS!

chant can become hypnotic after a while, stirring emotions in both speaker and listener. Today, chants are still prevalent in songs, prayers, demonstrations, and various forms of pop psychology.

DO-IT-YOURSELF CHANT:

Repeating the following phrase ten times a day in front of the mirror is a form of chant poetry:

"I'm here. I'm _____ . I love myself!"
               (positive adjective)

Cinquain—

Popularized by poet Adelaide Crapsey, the cinquain is a poem with five lines and a specific syllable count per line: two, four, six, eight, and two. Crapsey's poems "Triad" and "Laurel in the Berkshires" are the best-known of the poems in which she uses the cinquain rhythm to express a single thought or image.

DO-IT-YOURSELF CINQUAIN:

I Am

_____ Profound
   (two-syllable noun)

_____ , _____ , _____ , and _____
(one-syllable adj.) (two-syllable adj.) (one-syllable adj.)   (one-syllable adj.)

Challenging _____ and Tempting _____
            (one-syllable plural noun)   (one-syllable noun)

I Am

115

Confessional— A confessional poem goes directly to the heart of the poet's problems or behavior. Confessional poetry usually deals with difficult issues such as depression, addiction, or victimization. Famed poets of this genre include Anne Sexton, Sylvia Plath, and Robert Lowell. In *ANGST!*, "Perfect" by Kari Myers (page 25), "Who Are You?" by Tatiana "Sunshine" Farrow (page 26), and "Untitled" by SugarStar (page 96) are several examples of confessional poetry.

Conversational— A conversational poem is written in a casual style, as if the poet is talking to someone. *ANGST!*'s opener, "Etiquette of Dreams" by Myrita Craig (page 2), best sums up this genre.

Elegy— The elegy was created as a song of mourning in ancient Greece. It was first made popular in Greek tragedies, but it can cross over into themes that concern various forms of sorrow—not just ones related to death. Walt Whitman's "When Lilacs Last in the Dooryard Bloom'd," Rainer Maria Rilke's *Duino Elegies*, and Anne Sexton's "Sylvia's Death" are all examples of contemporary forms of elegies. For an *ANGST!* example of an elegy, check out Mabyn E. Ludke's "Party" (page 18).

Epic— An epic is a poem with a long narrative about a hero. Epics are often divided into cantos, which are like chapters in a book. Classical epics include: Homer's *Iliad*, Virgil's *Aeneid*, and Dante's *Divine Comedy*. Contemporary forms of epic poetry include: Allen Ginsberg's "Howl," T. S. Eliot's *The Waste Land*, and Jeana Mitchell's "Players" (page 14) of *ANGST!*. They all pass along a history, while teaching a moral lesson and inspiring the audience to take control of their destiny.

Epitaphs— Epitaphs are commemorations created for people's gravestones. They can mock or praise the deceased.

DO-IT-YOURSELF EPITAPH:

_____
(name)

_____
(dates)

Here lies _____.
(name)

What a _____ example of human _____.
(adjective) (noun)

Throughout _____ life,
(pronoun)

_____ gave all the _____ and
(name) (noun)

_____ that one can give.
(noun)

_____ will be missed by _____.
(name) (name(s))

Oh, what _____ we all feel.
(noun)

Free Verse— Known as _vers libre_ in French, this is poetry that just flows out in the heat of passion. It follows no rules; it is just raw intensity spilling on the page. Popular contemporary free-verse writers include: Charles Bukowski, e. e. cummings, Karen Finley, and Jack Kerouac. Some free-verse styles in _ANGST!_: "Creed" by Jessica M. Tisron (page 60) and "Nothing" by Tabi, Tribal Warrior (page 61).

Ghazal— This Persian poetry form has an Arabic name meaning "the talk of boys and girls," or "flirty words." The ghazal was originally formed by five to twelve couplets, with the poet's name included in the final couplet, and themes focused on love and booze. Between 1100 and 1500, the ghazal's Golden Age, the form was updated. The name of the poet was discarded, as was the rhyming, and themes shifted to the philosophical or mystical. Famed poets of the ghazal genre include: Rumi, Hafiz, Sanai, and Jami.

Haiku— Japanese in origin, haikus are poems inspired by nature, and written with sounds and rhythm in mind. Mastered by poets Matsuo Bashō, Yosano Buson, and Kobayashi Issa, haikus are meant to be simple-sounding, but profoundly meaningful. Haikus are written with a very formal structure of syllables—the most common form consists of three lines, the whole poem containing seventeen syllables, following this pattern: five syllables in the first line, seven in the second, and five in the third.

If thou pronounce curses and maledictions, I will say prayers.
The bitter answer seems beautiful on thy sugar-eating ruby lips.
—Hafiz

TRY SOME ANCIENT GHAZAL
FOR YOUR NEXT PICK-UP LINE!

DO-IT-YOURSELF HAIKU:

Memories _____ _____,
         (one-syllable verb)   (one-syllable adverb)

A _____ of distorted _____
   (one-syllable noun)   (one-syllable plural noun)

Too _____ to _____ _____ .
    (one-syllable adjective)   (one-syllable verb) (one-syllable adverb)

Imitation— Poems translated from foreign languages are "imitations"—but knowing a foreign language takes a backseat in this method. Created by American poet Robert Lowell, the genre took shape as he was working on a collection of translated poems. Upon realizing his translations were creating new poems altogether, he named the new genre and his book *Imitations*. It's perfect for sufferers of writer's block. Just pick up any foreign book, and go nuts.

Limerick— Usually five lines long, limericks are rhymed humorous poems that often feature a dirty twist. The structure of a limerick is very standard: lines one, two, and five all contain three beats and rhyme, and lines three and four contain two beats and rhyme. Edward Lear, author of the *Book of Nonsense*, was the first to establish the limerick as a tool of comedic verse.

List Poem— A poem that lists qualities of one object or thought, with or without rhyme, is a list poem. Considered an old form of poetry, the method still thrives in contemporary works. Father of surrealism André Breton's "Free Union," *ANGST!*'s Sarah Ston's "The Freak's Thoughts" (page 11) and Marissa Berlin's "If" (page 57) are all list poems.

119

Lune— A lune is like a haiku in that it is a three-line rhythmic poem. However, the syllabic pattern is different. The first line is five syllables; the second is three syllables; and the third is five syllables. Invented in the 1960s by poet Robert Kelly, the lune was Kelly's way of adapting the haiku for Western use. Realizing the English use fewer syllables than the Japanese in speech, he reformed the syllabic structure of the haiku to make the lune. With only thirteen syllables, the genre was named lune for the number of lunar months in a year. Subsequently, to get his style going, Kelly released a series of lunes entitled *Knee Lunes*.

DO-IT-YOURSELF LUNE:

_____ the _____
    (two-syllable verb)   (two-syllable noun)

release comes

_____ becomes _____
    (two-syllable noun)   (one-syllable adjective)

Lyric— Poems that are created to be sung along to music, or are songlike, are lyric poems. Sarah D. Bolam's "The Rock Revolution" (page 12), Babelicious's "Life Sucks" (page 29), and Julie Goodman's "Blah" (page 86) of *ANGST!* are all modern examples of this ancient Greek method.

Ode— A poem inspired by or written for a person, object, or occurrence is an ode. In ancient Greece and Rome, where this form originated, odes were meant to be sung. Today, an ode can be spoken or sung—like jessiKah dragon's "Ode to a Narcissist" (page 35) or Ashley Burkett's "Dear Pat" (page 45) of *ANGST!*

Prose Poem— A sonorous and rhythmic poem written in complete sentences, but without line breaks or meter. Nineteenth-century poet Aloysius Bertrand's "Gaspard of the Night" is an early example of prose poetry in the literary world. However, it was Charles Baudelaire's collection *Paris Spleen* that brought acclaim to the style and therefore provided the inspiration for nineteenth-century teen poetry prodigy Arthur Rimbaud's collection *A Season in Hell*. Today, the tradition carries on in *ANGST!* with Krista Marie Roll's "Me" (page 55) and Izzy's "Untitled" (page 77).

Quatrain— A stanza made up of four lines, this is the most common verse structure in poetry. One of eighteenth-century poet William Blake's most famous poems, "The Tyger," is a prime example of the use of quatrains. Despite its eighteenth-century heyday, the quatrain is still a popular mode of poetry, as demonstrated in *ANGST!*'s Dragana N. Bijedić's "Don't Screw Up" (page 20) and Crea's "Your Effect on Me" (page 34).

Rap— Despite the newness of this poetic genre, rap's influences stretch back through the Caribbean and the South to its origins in African oral storytelling traditions. Fusing strong traditional rhythmic beats with modern stories, rap's evolution began with the house and block parties throughout urban areas of New York's tri-state area in the 1970s. Among the first to bring rap to the forefront of popular culture were Grandmaster Flash, the Sugarhill Gang, and Run DMC. In creating rap, the rapper must consider rhythm, the tone of her or his musical backdrops, and rhymes.

Ritual Poem— Written for use in ceremonies, ritual poems help the orator gain a feeling of control over her or his life, by requesting help from forces of nature, strength from the beyond, or luck. The Jewish prayer for the dead, "Kaddish," Catholicism's "Act of Contrition," and the Alaskan Eskimos' "Storm Ritual" are all examples of this genre.

DO-IT-YOURSELF RITUAL POEM:

_____ , _____ hereby denounce you,
   (noun)   (pronoun)

Cast you back to the wretched _____
                                 (noun)

Where your _____ will crumble,
            (noun)

Faltering beneath _____ .
                (noun)

_____ shall destroy all your _____
(same pronoun)   (noun)

And _____ you forever to _____ .
     (verb)   (noun)

Skeltonic Verse— Named after its creator, English poet John Skelton (1460–1529), skeltonic poems have short lines— averaging three to six words per line, with a jumpy, herky-jerky beat and unpredictable rhyme scheme. The form was created as a rebellion against all the elaborate poetry of the time and was meant to breathe a new and spontaneous feeling into poetry. Allen Ginsberg utilizes skeltonics in his poem "Jumping the Gun on the Sun," and it is also hinted at in parts of *ANGST!*'s "Streamed 'Ode' Consciousness" by Jet Dennie (page 62).

Sonnet— Invented in the fourteenth century, the sonnet is heralded as the most popular of the poetic forms. Consisting of fourteen lines that follow rigid rules of rhyme and meter, the genre's most famous examples are Shakespeare's collection of love sonnets. *ANGST!*'s "Why Would He Want You?" by Amanda Kay Robertson (page 46) comes close to sonnet form.

Tanka— A tanka is a Japanese five-line poem that creates a mood. Made famous by poets Ki no Tsurayuki and Yosano Akiko, tanka themes lean more toward the depressing. Its format is usually short lines for the first and third lines; and longer second, fourth, and fifth lines.

DO-IT-YOURSELF TANKA:

Morning Mourning

Sunshine breaks _____, a painful reminder of
    (noun)

_____ begins.
 (sad emotion, noun)

Daybreak Daggers

My head is _____ and my hands begin to _____ .
   (adjective)   (verb)

Why does this _____ _____ infest me again?
    (sad emotion, noun) (adverb)

IN ANCIENT GREECE, A POET LAUREATE WOULD BE ADORNED WITH WREATHS OF LAUREL LEAVES. TODAY, POETS ARE CALLED POP STARS, AND THEY RECEIVE CADILLACS, WHICH FEATURE LAUREL WREATHS IN THEIR HOOD ORNAMENTS.

I'M THERE! WHERE'S THE POETRY?

You're now feeling the passion of life flowing through you, and you've got your tools for poetic articulation—but once you hit that blank sheet of paper, nothing comes out except mental dribble. What to do? Accept that genius isn't always quick, and remember that even the masters of our art have suffered through the pain of getting what is in their head and heart out onto the page articulately. Fret not, there are many ways for you to bring on a deluge of genius.

First, understand that everything is prewriting. Second, keep practicing what makes you open and grow, whether it is keeping a journal, meditating, photography, shopping, or imagining you are having a torrid love affair with your crush du jour. Relaxing and getting in tune with what's inside of you is essential in letting the magic flow. Third, remember that everything you do, see, taste, touch, hear, and feel is valid for expression—it's just that not everything can drive you to the edge of absolute inspiration. Fourth, keep track of all your feelings, thoughts, memories, hopes, fears, etc. They may not help you today, but someday they may inspire you to create a masterpiece. Finally, accept your greatness and power to overcome any obstacles. Know that you are the master of your destiny! To remind yourself of your strength, list three examples of excellence for yourself. Write about three challenges you have overcome and how you accomplished them. Remember, you're a genius—and a fabulous one too!

1. _____

2. _____

3. _____

GO!

Ready to set the world on fire with your inspirational creations? Sure you are! Just wanting and knowing you can is all the oomph you need. Keep in mind the following tidbits and you'll be fine!

- Everyone is a poet. Choose to be one, and you will be glad!
- Poetry is life, and appreciating your perspective is what being a poet is all about.
- Everything you think and feel is valid to express.
- Getting out your emotions is good, and the only way for positive growth.
- It takes practice to perfect any art form.
- If it feels good, and makes you better, do it—as long as it keeps you out of jail and happy!
- Repeat: "I'm a genius—and a fabulous one, too!"

ADD YOUR OWN MANTRAS:

_____

_____

_____

_____

_____

_____

_____

_____

_____

THE WHO'S WHO OF ANGST!

* POET LAUREATES *

ASHLEY BURKETT, Scorpio, Maryland

I'm originally from Florida, but now in Maryland. When I graduate, I plan to move back to Florida and go to college to study either psychology or interior design. I plan to live with my boyfriend for a year in between high school and college.

AMBER NICOLE LUPIN, Pisces, California

My only goal in writing is to express myself—not to make money or gain recognition (although that would be nice). If I couldn't write, I'd have to do interpretive dance.

APES, Aries, New Hampshire

I love math and science, but to really relax, I write poetry. I hope to become a chemical engineer someday, and deal with world issues. Most of all, thanks to Aunt Lydia for always telling me I can be what I want to be.

BABELICIOUS, Scorpio, England

I wrote "Life Sucks" for my hardcore band that is going to rule the world! We're tentatively called Piss and S***, but we're still deciding—look for me anyway! . . . . Yes, I am the hottie in pink fishnets with killer pipes!!!!!!!!!!

MARISSA BERLIN, Florida

DRAGANA N. BIJEDIĆ, Aquarius and proud!, Canada

I am originally from the former Yugoslavia (Bosnia and Herzegovina), now in Canada, I'm known to be pretty much laid back, yet outgoing and daredevilish. My poetic inspiration had me writing poems for a while, and many believe that I'll be into arts and literature. However, I see myself in computers, designing clothes, or perhaps teaching. I would teach ESL (English as a Second Language). I learned English five years ago, and ESL helped.

SARAH D. BOLAM, Pisces, New Jersey

I'm a rocker who adores the Smashing Pumpkins. I enjoy hanging out with friends, meeting retro people, playing guitar, and I love to laugh. I hope to become a famous journalist, so watch out!

JENNIFER BREWSTER, Cancer, California

My favorite thing to do is ride horses, and I love animals. I would like to be a horse trainer, and maybe do lessons for kids. I'm a people person, and I love my boyfriend.

CORTNEY A. CALIGUR, Capricorn, Indiana

I hope to graduate from college with a degree in writing, and write books for young adults. I have written a few books already, with my own illustrations. Nobody else has read them, because I write more for my own amusement.

BETHANN CLEARY, Aries, North Carolina

MYRITA CRAIG, Libra, Ohio

I am a fourteen-year-old girl who has realized that life isn't just a walk in the park. It's a difficult world out there, and we girls have to stick together. I am happy to share my words with you so that we all know we are the future and we are beautiful.

CREA, Aries, Nebraska

I'd like to get my work (musical or literary) out in the public. My voice hasn't been heard for all my life, and I think having the whole world hear it would appease me. Aside from writing, I play the violin and piano infernally.

LAUREN K. DANEK, Taurus, Pennsylvania

Hey! My name is Lauren, and I just want to give a shout-out to all my friends—luv you guys—and my family! Luv and sunshine! L8a!

RACHEL DANIELLO, Libra, Maryland

I'll be graduating from high school in June 2001, and I hope to become a novelist, journalist, and editor after I graduate from college. I rarely write poetry. The poem "I Have to Be Me" is lighthearted. It is a true-to-life poem that encourages people to be true to themselves and to avoid conforming to standards set by others.

JET DENNIE, Capricorn, Virginia

I would love to dedicate my poem to Larry, a.k.a. Ranius, and Erica, a.k.a. One Who Can Move Her Eyebrows Independently of Each Other.

ALISON DENNO, Pisces, Michigan

Hi. My name's Ali (Alison). I'm pretty much like all of you out there. I run track; dance tap, jazz, and ballet; play soccer; and I'm a cheerleader. I wrote "Feet" in sixth grade for a poetry festival, and I'd just like to say thanks to Mrs. Beechuk for being such a great teacher.

JESSIKAH DRAGON, Gemini, Idaho

jessiKah plays the cello, makes excellent birthday cakes, and wants to be a rock star. She adores mix tapes, shows, maraschino cherries, e. e. cummings, and Audrey Hepburn. The soundtrack to her life includes Weezer, Modest Mouse, Björk, The Impossibles, Self, The Juliana Theory, and that dog.

TATIANA "SUNSHINE" FARROW, Pisces, Georgia

I speak fairly fluent French and have been playing the violin for five years. I plan to attend Duke University in 2002. I love art, music, Shakespeare, and playing Twister.

REBECCA FURNELL, Virgo, Canada

KAREN GATHANY, Sagittarius, Alabama

Hi! I'm fourteen. I play the guitar, and I love it. I also enjoy designing websites on the Internet, and hanging out with my friends. I have no idea where life will take me, but I guess I will find out someday.

JULIE GOODMAN, Virgo, California

Originally from South Orange, NJ, but currently in California. I enjoy writing poems and songs, playing guitar, soccer, chilling with friends, and partying. One of my wishes was to get some poems published and touch people's lives with them (even if it's by making them laugh hysterically for hours).

LIBBY GUNTER, Pisces, Montana

I want to go to law school and become a successful lawyer. My hobbies consist of poem writing and photography. I want to thank my wonderful parents, and especially my sister Aubrey, for believing in me.

DAITVIA HOLBRIONA, Libra, Oregon

Advice for the world—just be happy and live your life, because life is beautiful. Love is what holds us together in perfect unity.

IZZY, Scorpio, Louisiana

My poem was written for a boy who did me wrong, and made me feel like %@$&! I have since learned that he is the loser for using me like he did. As for all those others who have done me wrong, HA-HA!!!! My poem is in a book, and yours is not!

L, Scorpio, New Jersey

We all get angry, and when we do, we should exert our energy in more positive ways. Even though a poem can't fix anything that's gone wrong, it still helps us to calm down and gives us a healthier mental state. In this world, it's most important for people to be able to control their anger and smile a little bit more.

JESSICA LAUNDERVILLE, Pisces, Ohio

I would like to say I wrote that poem for a guy I love with all my heart. We are together still, and plan to be for a while. I love you, Cory.

LAUREN, Taurus, South Dakota

I like to play soccer, and shop, like normal girls. I like the Internet and hanging out with my friends. I like to pull pranks on ppl too. I am very sarcastic and say anything that is on my mind. I like going to watch sporting events and am a pretty good student. I wanna say hi to Jen, Di, Sarah, Megan, Libby, Taylor, Joni, Steph, Riley, and yer mom. . . . Dats it.

ASHLEY N. LORENZI, Leo, Ohio

I'm just an 18-year-old red-headed and brown-eyed little girl. I've had a lot of shitty times with guys, but I've now learned and found a wonderful one. I'd like to thank all the assholes that have inspired me in my poetry.

MABYN E. LUDKE, Aries, New York

I feel very honored to have this chance to influence others through my creativity.

JEANA MITCHELL, Cancer, Oregon

ERICA MORGAN, Gemini, Ohio

I would like to dedicate this poem to the love of my life, Brad Chance. Thank you for everything that you have done for me. I love you with all of my heart and soul.

KARI MYERS, Taurus, Virginia

Basically, I love to create things. I draw, paint, write, and do things of that nature. That's what I'm good at, what I live for, and what I hope to do for the rest of my life.

HEATHER E. NYHOF, Taurus, California

I am a very independent and strong-willed person. I will be a freshman at UC Santa Barbara, pursuing a B.A. in English this year, where I hope to find happiness, friends, and a chance to publish some of my other work.

BRITTNEY PALMER, Scorpio, Arkansas

My greatest passion is dancing. I want to become a professional dancer and perform on MTV videos. I also hope to get a big break and become a famous actress someday on the big screen!

BECKY PEYTON, Sagittarius, Kentucky

Hi. My name is Becky Peyton, and I am a sixteen-year-old. I enjoy talking to people, listening to music, dancing, and helping out others. One of these days, I hope to marry the man of my dreams, have two children, and be a first-grade teacher.

QUEEN B, Libra, New York

I will probably grow up to be a freaky cat lady, but I don't care. I'll have lots of unconditional love in my life. In the meantime, I plan to go to college abroad.

JESSICA J. RATLIFF, Libra, Ohio

Student at Xavier University, majoring in history and professional education. I write to ease the pain and to let others get to know me.

HANNAH RICHARDS, Gemini, Vermont

I am amazed by life, art, music, writing, movies, and good food. I see beauty all around me, and I love being outside. I want to major in visual art and creative writing/English, then minor in philosophy. I believe that everyone can, and should, do at least one thing to make the world a more beautiful and better place.

AMANDA KAY ROBERTSON, Capricorn, Idaho

I am currently a senior at Jefferson Alternative High School. After I graduate, I would like to go to college and become a psychiatrist. I would like to thank my family for helping me through the hardest times of teenage life.

KRISTA MARIE ROLL, Aries, Montana

I love to laugh and make people laugh. I suppose you could say that's my hobby. Hopefully, someday my dreams of being a financial advisor will come true. I love to play tennis, and my favorite weekend activity is to watch the latest new movie release.

RAISSA MAE SAGUN, Aries, Canada

I began experimenting with poetry at eleven, and by the time I was thirteen, it became a way of self-expression. I also have a passion for music, basketball, and—well, life. In the future, I hope to be a successful pediatrician.

SARAH STON, Virgo, Illinois

SUGARSTAR, Sagittarius, England
I want to ride an elephant through Thailand, meditate with the Pharaohs, eat crepes on the Champs-Elysées, swim with the Alaskan whales, dance at Carnival in Rio, drive a "doom" buggy across the moon, and be cute all the while!

REBECCA SULIN, Libra, Ohio

BETHANY SULLENS, Libra, Mississippi
My most favorite thing to do in life is to have fun. This includes *The Wizard of Oz, Rugrats* . . . and eating and sleeping! . . . And remember, always smile while talking on the phone. It makes you sound more pleasant.

ERICA SUTHERLAND, Gemini, Massachusetts
I'm seventeen years old. For fun, I pretty much just chill with my friends. I like writing, acting, and most sports. In the future, I want to go to college in NY, and I hope to become an actress.

TABI, TRIBAL WARRIOR, Gemini, North Carolina
I am a child of God, a.k.a. Tribal Warrior. My inspirations are the Lord up above and anyone who praises His name. My goal in life is to start a Christian band and spread the word of God.

GLENESSA TAYLOR, Taurus, Maryland
My ultimate life goal would be to reach people with my poems. It would be really cool to have them take something special from my words. I hope this poem does that.

JESSICA M. TISRON, Aquarius, Michigan
I live my life on experiences and learning. I love meeting new people. I hope to either become a writer or a child psychologist. Who knows, maybe both. Find yourself, love yourself, and when you do, you'll truly experience life. Love to those who created the experience and always hold a piece of my heart: Danny, Tommy, Chicory, Mary, Timmy, Katie, Luke, Laura, and my mommy!

DANIELLA MARIE VACCA, Virgo, New York
I'm sixteen, and I am a senior in high school. I don't know exactly what my plans are for the future, but I do know what I am interested in. I'm interested in fashion design, film, and dance. My only wishes for the future are to be happy and to love what I'm doing.

THERESA J. VANDERMEER, Aries, Michigan

When I am old enough to work, I hope to have a job where I can write. Besides writing, I enjoy traveling, snowboarding, playing volleyball, and hanging out with my friends. Thanks all, and props to PlanetKiki for the chance to write creatively and be noticed.

ANGELINE VUONG, Leo, Georgia

"Work like you don't need the money, dance like nobody is watching, and love like you've never been hurt." Live by these words, just like I do, and you'll be a very happy person.

AJA WATSON, Aries, Missouri

I have lived in five different states. I was born in WY, but I currently live in Missouri. I am my own person. I learned long ago that I can't truly be good at being someone I'm not. I live my life knowing that it could be long or short, so I take nothing for granted.

RESOURCES

FOR MORE ON POETIC STRUCTURE:

Abrams, M.H. *A Glossary of Literary Terms* (Fort Worth, TX: Harcourt Brace College Publishers, 1993, 1988, 1985, 1981, 1971, 1969, 1957, 1941).

Baldick, Chris. *The Concise Oxford Dictionary of Literary Terms* (Oxford, England: Oxford University Press, 1990).

Hafiz, translated by Yahya Monsterca.

Hunter, J. Paul. *The Norton Introduction to Poetry, Third Edition* (New York: W. W. Norton and Company, 1986, 1981, 1973).

Padgett, Ron, ed. *The Teachers and Writers Handbook of Poetic Forms* (New York: Teachers & Writers Collaborative, 1987).

THE SIGNS OF THE ZODIAC ASSOCIATED WITH POETRY ARE GEMINI, PISCES, AND LIBRA.

FIFTY-THREE PERCENT OF THE CONTRIBUTORS OF ANGST! WERE BORN UNDER ONE OF THESE STAR SIGNS. COINCIDENCE? YOU DECIDE!

FOR MORE ON SOME OF OUR POETS, LOG ON TO:

http://zeropumpkin.boltpages.com = Sarah D. Bolam
www.dork.com/jessikah = jessiKah dragon
www.playfullstar.pitas.com = Daitvia HolBriona
http://nymoae.boltpages.com/ = Mabyn Ludke
www.envy.nu/racy = Amber Nicole Lupin
www.geocities.com/triste6/ = Kari Myers

As for other places to look for poetry and inspirational thoughts besides PlanetKiki.com, the one-stop shop for illumination and fiesta, . . . Poetry is an inspiration that comes from the everyday—however fantastical or uneventful. So look around and see who and what has made yours the experience it has been and keep examining life and yourself to find more!

THANKS!

KAREN AND KIKI'S SPECIAL, SPECIAL THANKS GO TO:

Baudy (a.k.a. The Bauddha), Betty Tom, Elaine Tom, Garrett Tom, John Tom, Theresa and Chung Ping Tom, and even Uncle Peter, The Bauddhist Temple, Brenda and Zahra Bruno, Liz Carey, Keith Cuva, Rick Dause, Erika Fast, Julie Guarino, Mike Hemmings, Gillian Hettinger, Meena Hwang (Gina and Bora too), Monica Khanna, Margie Girl (a.k.a. Margarita Gaines), Alex Pastewski, Jaime Propp, Sarita Ramjit, Angela Ruddy, John Sampson, Christine Sauertieg, Chris Shaw, Arion SoRelle, Mina Takata, Angelika Velez, and a zillion kisses to Matt Frost!!!

MATT FROST'S HUGE THANKS GO TO:

Karen Tom; Kiki; Geoff Seelinger; Foomedia.com; Fondue Media; Michael, Susan, and Miriam Frost; Don and Marie Creviere; Bernard and Mina Frost; Donald and Jane Seelinger; Pico, Monika, and Martin Baumert; Matt Campbell; Lori Beyer; Grazyna Jankowski; Trent Hanson; Roswitha Mueller; Andrew Horn; Maggie Dietz; Jack Davidson; Mike Rosenberg; Ross Ortner; and Eric Baum.

ALSO, THANKS TO ALL THE POETS THAT MADE THIS BOOK KICK-ASS, AND TO ALL THE GIRLS OF PLANETKIKI.COM WHO ARE ALSO KICK-ASS!